I0669188

DAUGHTER OF HADES
ENGAGED
BOOK TWO

FoxTales Press

DANI HOOTS

Engaged
Daughter of Hades, #2
© 2018 FoxTales Press
Content and line edits by Justin Boyer
2nd Cover Design Copyright © 2019 by Biserka
Designs
1st Cover Design Copyright © 2016 by Desiree
DeOrto
Formatting by Dani Hoots
All rights reserved.

ISBN: 978-1-942023-50-0

Chapter 1

Chrys

I lay there in my bed, listening to *Hanging* On by Falling in Reverse. I could stay here forever and let time waste away until the wedding. I could just stare up at the posters I had of different bands I liked—the bands that Huntley had introduced me to.

Placing my arm over my eyes, I tried to push back the tears. I was stronger than this, I knew, but damn it still hurt to realize how much I lost in such a short time frame. For hundreds of years I was living down here in the Underworld, never caring about what happened on the surface. Then finally I snapped at Persephone, and I just had to know.

What was up there that was so damn important?

I knew I shouldn't blame her as this was all my fault. It was my decision to go to Earth and disobey Father's direct orders. I should have listened to him, and I should have listened to Huntley. He knew it was a terrible idea from the start, but he stayed by my side to make sure I remained safe.

And now Huntley was gone.

The realization that I wouldn't ever see him again came back to me and the tears made their way down the sides of my face. Damn it, I shouldn't have thought about it all again. This was literal torture.

No, what was to come would be torture.

Because of my mistake, because I was a fool who didn't listen to what her father said, I would have to marry Zeus, a god who wanted to see my destruction and wanted to watch my father suffer. On top of that, he was known for his affairs, his illegitimate (and legitimate) children, and just causing a lot of trouble all around. He was the God of Gods, Ruler of Olympus, and he got to do pretty much whatever he wanted, and my brief time on Earth definitely taught me that. I had stepped into the big family drama, how lucky was I?

Now Father wasn't speaking to me, and I doubted I would win his trust back. I had always thought he was overprotective, just thinking that something horrible would happen because he worried too much. Apparently I was wrong, since something did in fact happen.

And it threw my entire world into the gutter. Between Huntley being gone, having AJ betray me after hundreds of years of friendship, and Father giving me the cold shoulder, none of my life would ever be back to normal. Then, in a few months, I would be married to Zeus and… I didn't even want to think of what would ha*ppen next.*

*Baby, I adore you, but this ain't gonna la*st forever.

I rubbed my face dry and got up out of my bed. It was still morning at least, but probably a lot later than when I should have gotten up. I theoretically was supposed to help Father with judging since Persephone was gone, although he hadn't been too strict about it lately. It was my duty, though, I would be there when she was away, condemning souls with Father. At least I would never have to see Persephone's face again. I wondered if she even cared.

Father wasn't too happy about how much Persephone pushed me into leaving. Although I didn't blame her after everything that had happened, knowing it was my selfish desire that led me to Earth, Father hadn't come to that conclusion yet. He blamed her for most of it. It was because of her magical rings we had used to travel between worlds; it was her dragging men down here, talking constantly about how much she hated it here that made him lose his daughter. At least, that's what I heard him yell at her on more than one occasion. There were countless nights where they kept me awake, crying under the covers as they argued just as she left. I hadn't seen him this mad at her since, well, ever. However, I've seen Mother mad at Father many times over. So I guess it was only fair.

Changing into some simple black clothes, skinny jeans,

a tank, and boots, I threw my hair back and stared at myself in the mirror. I finally understood why my father always wore black—it definitely fit the mood lately. Although we sometimes could stand being in the same room with each other, that didn't mean he really spoke to me, at least not like he used to. So it felt darker here than it ever did before. Gods could hold grudges and I wasn't looking forward to how long this atmosphere was going to last.

Deciding to grab some breakfast, I strolled down the hallways, taking my time since I didn't necessarily want to help judge souls at that moment. The entire castle was pretty quiet, especially after everything that had happened. I had always grown up thinking they were so silent, but now with everyone gone and being somewhat neglected by Hades, I now knew what real silence was like. And it sucked.

I still had my puppy Cerberus, at least, and spoiled him rotten. If he wasn't with Father right now, he would be following me around, wanting to play. I had gathered some bones for him last night and couldn't wait to watch as his many heads fought over who got to chew the bone first.

I could tell he missed Huntley, as he liked to mess with the human. Most people were automatically afraid of him, and Huntley at first was pretty terrified. But he warmed up to Cerberus, and Cerberus took advantage of that. At least injuries here healed pretty quickly, as everyone here was already dead.

So right now I was alone. After all these years I

thought I was fine with being alone, as there weren't many people who wanted to hang out with the daughter of Hades, but I realized I was wrong. I hadn't known true loneliness until now.

I got closer with the chef recently, since he prepared my meals and put them aside without Father knowing. Hades didn't like that I had been sleeping in and told the chef to stop making me meals late in the morning. It was really petty of Father, but I felt bad when the chef got everything back out to make me something. So we decided it would be best to just make me something and put it in the fridge. I could at least reheat it.

The head chef most recently was a man named Vincenzo from a small town in Italy, where apparently the best chefs lived, at least according to Persephone. Then Father gave him the option to stay and be a chef for a few months or so and then he could go to Elysian Fields. Would anyone pass up an offer like that?

I snuck into the kitchen, trying not to distract any of the other chefs and Vincenzo as they were preparing lunch. Had I really slept in that long? I checked the clock. Yup, it was almost eleven. Vincenzo glanced over to me and waved with a smile. I waved back and mouthed a 'thank you', especially since he shouldn't have to deal with a lazy goddess like me.

Opening the fridge, I found the plate with some Egg Florentine. It looked delicious. Vincenzo always had the most flavorful of florentines I had ever had. This one had artichoke, roasted garlic, caramelized onions, and sun-dried tomatoes.

I swiftly put it in the oven and let it heat as I fumbled around with the tea kettle. Ever since I went to England, I had been craving Earl Grey tea. I liked having it every morning as it woke me up and gave me just enough energy to get through the day without giving me the jitters. Just as the kettle was done, and the tea had steeped, the Florentine was ready to go. I grabbed it and retreated into the dining hall.

I never understood why the dining hall was so large when there was theoretically only three of us. It was pretty grand too, with scrolls hanging on the wall, mainly weaved landscapes of the Underworld. Mother always hated them and sometimes threw drinks at them when she was angry. As for the table, it was a long, ebony wood table with a dark gray liner. It could sit probably fifty people at this table, if not more. For centuries we have never had guests down here.

It suddenly hit me—was it because no one could find out I existed? Did Father have more people visiting before I was born? Was I the reason he was alone here?

I don't know why it never occurred to me before now, with all this grandeur that encompassed the castle, that maybe it was for guests besides the deceased. Maybe Father gave all that up just for me. And that was why me leaving made him feel so much more betrayed than just a simple disobedient act.

Sitting down, I clapped my hands together and said," thank you for the meal!" and dug straight in. There was no point in thinking about what life was like before I was around anymore—especially since now he could go back to that lifestyle, as the secret of my existence was out in the open.

I figured I would have the dining hall alone for a while, especially since it was between meals, but as I was halfway through my breakfast, the door to the main hallway opened. I glanced up to find Hades standing there. I jumped up out of my chair, almost choking on my food in the process. I coughed, trying to get it back up or force it down.

"Did I startle you?" he asked with almost no hint of emotion. It was the same tone he had every time he talked to me. It was worse than when he didn't talk to me. I couldn't tell what kind of things he was thinking when he spoke like that. Was it hatred? Resentment? Frustration? I didn't know and had a feeling I would never find out.

I nodded. "Yeah, I figured you would be working." Which was the truth, as that was all he did most of the day. Even though that was his job in the Underworld, it felt like he had been working more than normal lately.

"I was working, and you were supposed to be too, or have you forgotten your duties?"

I finally got the peace of artichoke down and coughed once more to clear anything else in my throat. "Yeah, well, I woke up late."

"And so you figured you would just skip out on the entire day?"

Shrugging, I didn't answer his question. Yeah, I had been hoping I could skip ,especially since he had been giving me the cold shoulder as I sat there and watched the Three Stooges, the three judges that helped him with handling all the dead. I liked calling them that because they weren't the sharpest knives in the light sockets sometimes. They had been assigned by Zeus to make sure Hades was doing his job, as if he wasn't trustworthy. I guess when you were a lying piece of shit god, you just expected all the other gods to be the same.

Father ended the awkward silence between us. "Well, I need you to help me."

"Can I finish eating at least?" I asked, gesturing to the meal I was in the middle of eating.

He glanced to my plate of food. "What did I tell you about making Vincenzo cook you something so late in the morning?"

Damn it, he remembered. "He didn't, he just leaves leftovers and I reheat it."

"And what did I tell you about reheating a chef's food?"

I sighed. "That it's rude and I should wake up on time when it's fresh."

"Exactly. We will discuss this later. Now hurry up."

Hades stood there, not leaving the room like I expected him to.

"Are… are you waiting here for me?" I asked.

"Yes, now hurry it up."

I quickly downed the rest of my food, which I thought was more disrespectful to Vincenzo than reheating it, but that wasn't going to be a conversation Father and I would be having. If I tried to point out any of his faults lately, I got my head bitten off. It was better to just to not say anything.

Chapter 2

<u>Huntley</u>

This wasn't fair.

I wanted to take my anger out on something—*I nee*ded to take my anger out on something. I was never one to stay still, and it always led to someone handing me a hit or sniff or bottle. That was the old me, though, and there was no way I would be that person again—not when so much was at stake.

But I needed to get this energy out, whether it be on a person or inanimate object was still up in the air. If I could find AJ I just might take it out on a person. I couldn't kill him, I knew, but I could do my best to make him suffer.

He disappeared the moment he was given immortality

though, knowing some of us would come after him, mainly me. Hades probably would have if he didn't have other things to worry about, such as trying to stop this marriage between his daughter and Zeus.

Which was also what I was doing.

Pothos had bought me a fidget spinner because I couldn't sit still. Apparently gods were good at wasting time because they didn't seem to be that worried. I broke it within a day and then threw it into the wall. On an unrelated note, it was possible to put a hole in the wall with one of those things. Pothos wasn't too happy about that.

I was still worried, as we had made little progress in finding a way to help Chrys out. Supposedly Prometheus was trying to figure something out, but I didn't know if he was that honest or not. The moment Zeus showed up, Prometheus disappeared. I didn't think he would come back after everything was said and done. Apparently that belief was wrong since he came back to help.

It made me wonder if he was distracting us for Zeus, making sure we don't make a move against him. Pothos kept telling me that was paranoia, but I felt like my paranoia so far has been correct, mainly about AJ and coming to Earth.

So at the moment I was at Pothos' place, staying with him since I had no place to go. I was surprised he offered, since we didn't exactly have the greatest first meeting. He had tried to sleep with Chrys and while it still irked me, I could understand it. She had such a different godly power radiating off of her compared to all the other goddesses. She was practically irresistible.

Pacing back and forth in the living area of the flat, I noticed that I had , in fact, worn part of the rug down. Pothos had warned me about that and told me to stop walking in that spot, but I couldn't help it—I had too much energy in my body.

The front door clicked unlocked and swung open. I stopped my pacing and jumped to the other side of the room. If he saw me standing in my worn-out area of the rug, I would get chewed out again. I was here without having to pay after all.

Pothos and Mel stepped in. They were two gods that had been alive for who knew how long, yet still went to high school. I didn't get it, but then again I was human. I guess they just really craved more drama, or maybe they thought human drama was a lot more fun than that of their world. But in reality Pothos probably just went because he was trying to get away from Mel, and Mel went to follow Pothos.

Pothos glanced over at me and I gave him a sarcastic smile. He rolled his eyes.

"What did I tell you about pacing in that spot?" he said as he threw his stuff on the couch.

"I can't help it, I need to get out of this flat."

Mel placed her bag on the dining table and wrapped her arms around Pothos. "Then come join us at school. It's a lot of fun."

"No," both Pothos and I said in unison. I actually tried that one day. It didn't end well, and I got detention for a week. Besides, sitting still and hearing adults try to teach me things they didn't even know about really pissed me off, on top of all the teenagers who just wanted to fuck with each other, both mentally and physically.

Though dealing with the gods from Greek Mythology wasn't much different from high school.

"Sorry I asked," Mel said, grinning. "I could manipulate your sense of time and let you see your greatest fear and let you live it over again and again?"

Mel, short for Melinoe, was the Goddess of Ghosts, so she liked to torture people mentally. She could put you in your own little hell for however long you wanted. She was the daughter of Persephone and Zeus, who was disguised as Hades at the time. As I said, the Greek gods were all like high-schoolers with way too much power.

So technically she was Chrys' half-sister, which was really weird. However, no other child was bore by Hades, which was why Chrys had so many people after her. Apparently there had been a legend of a child bore from Hades that could take down Olympus once and for all and out of fear, Zeus made it so Hades couldn't have children. Chrys was a miracle—a miracle that Hades hid until now.

Zeus tried to kill Chrys the moment he saw her, but Hades stopped him. Once Zeus took a moment to think about it, he decided he would rather take Chrys as his wife. Yeah, all the stories about Zeus were true, he did just think with his dick.

I answered Mel. "I'm good. I just need to get this energy out. I think I'm going to go for a run in a bit."

"You are crazy," Pothos exclaimed. "It's still fucking cold outside."

I shrugged. "Better than just sitting here and doing nothing. Might be cold, but at least this energy will be gone."

Pothos seemed hesitant for a moment, but said nothing. I knew what he was thinking though, and I didn't know how to reassure him without being straightforward. Both of us stood there, awkwardly, not able to actually communicate what we were thinking.

"Oh my goddess, just say it!" Mel laughed. "Pothos is worried you are going to try to send yourself to the Underworld again."

"I won't. I learned my lesson the first time."

As I said it, I didn't know what I meant by "the first time". Technically the first was when I had overdosed and actually died, and found in the Underworld by Chrys. However, what Pothos was referring to was after Chrys was taken to the Underworld, I had tried to overdose again and when that didn't work, tried to jump in front of a big truck. It wasn't that I wanted to die, but it was that I knew that was the only way I could get to the Underworld. It made sense to me, expect that apparently when one dies by killing one's self, they just float along the rivers of the Underworld until someone, such as Charon, finds them. It could be a few hours, it could be lifetimes.

So apparently Chrys had found me floating in the river and decided to drag me out of the water, lie about it to her father, and never told me. And AJ helped. I was a little pissed she never told me, but I supposed she figured I didn't want to talk about the way I died.

Pothos changed the subject. "You know, Prometheus will think of something. He always does. We still have time."

Great, this again. I shook my head. "It's been months already, it's past Christmas now for crying out loud! We have until September and it's not even nine months away. How has he not come up with anything? Where the hell is he anyway, we haven't seen his face for weeks!"

"Calm down and trust him, he knows what he is doing."

"What, because I'm a human and can't understand?"

Pothos took a seat on the couch, Mel sitting right up against him. He ignored her. "There's that, and we are much older and wiser than you, so just shut up."

"Hmph, whatever. I don't trust him anyway, so I think we should have a back-up plan."

Pothos raised an eyebrow. "You don't trust Prometheus?"

I shook my head. "No, not when he ran the moment we were in trouble."

"He has good reason to be afraid of Zeus. He was chained up and tortured for thousands of years. Not to mention he was the one who tried to get you three to safety before you were discovered. If it hadn't been for AJ, you all would have been fine."

I swore if I ever saw that prick again, I would beat the shit out of him, and make him wish he could die. He had used Chrys to come back to this world, and she could have even met the deadly fate of being completely destroyed, or sent to Tartarus for all of eternity. Was this world really worth all that? He was destined for Asphodel Fields, so it made little sense why he would want to come back to be a mortal. Whatever the reason may be, I definitely would try to kill him for threatening Chrys' survival while achieving his goal.

"And before you say that you are gonna kill that bastard, I know. You've said it a million times."

"Well I will kill him, or at least try."

"Nothing you do could kill him, though I understand your reasoning. He's long gone by now though, or at least I would think he would leave by now. This isn't where he's from. And he wanted to go back to his great kingdom, though his kingdom is under a bunch of buildings and dirt."

I wished I could see his face when he realized his entire kingdom was gone. We had told him that. "I'm still not sure if I trust Prometheus. He may have helped then, but he has no reason to help us now. He could just get into trouble again, and there is no up-side in this for him."

Pothos shrugged. "I mean, there is the satisfaction of not letting Zeus get away with something. I would do it just for that."

It seemed like a lot of these gods felt the same way about Zeus—they despised him. That, or they kissed his ass. Or both really. I just hoped that these gods wouldn't turn their back on me and suck up to Zeus when I would need them most.

"Whatever, I still don't trust him. I will wait though, since I have to. Meanwhile, I'm going to make back up plans."

Pothos waved his hand. "Whatever, you humans are so impatient. Do what you want, but just stop pacing before you permanently ruin my floor."

"Sorry we humans don't have an eternity to settle things. It makes us a bit impatient."

Pothos let out a brief laugh. "I'm really surprised Hades let you stay in the palace with an attitude like that."

"You think I would ever talk back to Hades? Though I don't understand why he really kept me around."

"Yes, you do, don't lie to yourself—you made his daughter smile. Of all the gods, he actually cares about his offspring, although mainly because she shouldn't exist in the first place."

We all had seen the extent of Chrys' powers when Poseidon had attacked her. That fight did not help her case as far as Zeus was concerned. Chrys had the power over life and death, and Zeus didn't think anyone should have such a power. We watched as she killed and revived Poseidon over and over again. It was... awesome.

"If only she could get back to the Underworld before Poseidon had noticed..." I whispered.

No one said anything, as we all agreed. None of this would have happened if it weren't for Poseidon, or actually his son AJ. But if we had just hurried a little faster...

"I'm going for my run. I'll be back in a couple of hours."

I turned for the door and left them before they could say anything else. I needed to clear my mind, figure out what to do next. Even if I had all of Olympus against me, I would never give up on the girl I loved.

Chapter 3

Chrys

Just as expected, Father and I didn't really speak much to each other. I sat there, listening to him talk but at the same time glancing around the throne room. It was mainly greyish-blue stone, bleak, and rather boring to be honest. I guess the God of the Underworld didn't want to make those who needed to be judged feel comfortable. It wouldn't be honest.

The thrones themselves were a darker grey, metallic looking, but quite comfortable. After centuries of having to sit here, it would make sense to have something that feels nice and cushioned.

The Three Stooges, Minos, Rhadamanthus, and Aeacus, however, always stood and circled the contestant. Today they seemed a little distracted, and I had a feeling it was because of the tension between Father and I. Neither of us could even make eye contact.

This was getting ridiculous. I needed to talk to him; I needed him to be my father again. I couldn't change the past, and neither could he. We had to make this work... somehow.

I wondered why Father even wanted me to sit here with him today, as it had been quite some time since he wanted my help, not that I was really helping. I was just sitting there, listening to him judge those who were on the fence between going either to Asphodel Meadows or to Tartarus. Even in his foul mood, he didn't let that impede his judgement. For that, I admired my father—he was able to disconnect his feelings from his job.

Now if he just did that when dealing with me.

"Tartarus." My father said, sentencing the woman who was before the stand now.

I watched as the woman's eyes widened, and Cerberus came galloping into the room. Cerberus did his job well and came every time when Father summoned him. He usually obeyed me, although sometimes he would take his time about it.

Cerberus had a lot of work today, though, as many of the people Father had judged were worthy of Tartarus. I didn't disagree with my father either, as he was level-headed when it came to work. It was interesting to watch their plea—to see their regret when they realized that the afterlife was real and everything that they did came at a price. I never could understand, even when they didn't know there was an afterlife, why they thought the things they did were okay—that there weren't any repercussions. I supposed on Earth sometimes the bad guy got away with that. Not here, though, as we could see everything the humans did.

As the woman screamed, one of the heads of Cerberus chomped down on her leg and ran off to dump her into Tartarus. Such a cute little puppy doing his job. I wished more people could see that, but I guess most people only saw him when he was dragging them off to eternal torment.

The Three Stooges didn't seem to mind Cerberus. In fact I have caught them giving him treats before. They tried not to show it for some reason, maybe because Persephone didn't care for the animal. Either way, it just showed me they were more caring than one would think, this being the underworld after all.

I wondered what Mother was like on Earth versus the way she was down here. Father always said she was much the same, full of drama just like all the other gods. She belonged there as far as I was concerned, and I didn't look forward to dealing with any of the other gods' drama that he had always spoke of. Then again, it was better than Tartarus.

Although many humans didn't think Tartarus existed, all the gods did and it was their greatest fear. When a god fell into Tartarus, there was no way that they would ever return, or at least a tiny percentage. Most of the Titans were in Tartarus, suffering for eternity, as that was where Zeus had sent them after the war. Only Zeus and

Hades could send gods to Tartarus, otherwise there probably would have been no gods left between arguments and such.

I didn't know of many, if any, gods that my father sent to Tartarus, whereas there was quite a few gods that Zeus had sent to be tortured for eternity. I would have been one of those gods, but luckily Father came in time to save me. He bought me enough time to get Zeus to change his mind and propose marriage instead, which was still an eternal punishment in reality. It was just a tad better, especially since I could spend most of the year in the Underworld.

Father didn't see it as being a blessing though, I could tell that just by the energy he had been giving off for the past four months. Gods were known for holding grudges and I just hoped that Father would calm down sometime soon. I couldn't deal with this tension any longer, especially since I did everything I could to make sure I could spend time with him while married to Zeus.

No other person entered the throne room, meaning we were done for the day. It felt like my heart was going to jump out of my chest because I had a feeling now Father would want to have "a talk".

"Well, that was the last one," Hades stated, almost zoning out. "Minos, Rhadamanthus, and Aeacus, please leave us."

I knew it. The Three Stooges each bowed and left my father and I alone. I wanted to run away, go hide somewhere in the castle, hope he wouldn't find me. But I couldn't run away from this conversation, not to mention

I wanted to finally come to terms with each other. Whether this conversation will come to that is another conversation.

In front of everyone, Father kept his posture and strength, and showed no signs of being tired or frustrated. I was one of the few he would show what he was thinking—his weariness of his job. He wasn't like the other gods, who could take a holiday off. He had to always be here. Leaning back in his throne, Father let out a sigh and rubbed his face. His coldness had left, which meant this would be an actual "talk".

We sat there in silence for a moment, which made my heart beat even faster. I could feel it resonate in my body as fear took hold. As to why I was so afraid, I wasn't sure.

"Tell me again why you thought it was a good idea to go up there," he finally said. "Because I keep replaying it again and again in my head and I don't see why you would ever make such a stupid decision. I thought you were smarter than this."

That was why my anxiety was at its peak—because I knew he would just blame me again. Even if he was asking me to say why, it didn't mean he would listen. He was just going to judge me and make me feel worse than I already did.

"Father, please, we have gone over this again and again. Why won't you just—"

"But you never answer me," he interrupted with a little more sternness in his voice. "What was so important that you risked everything that I had worked so hard in putting together to keep you safe from them?"

I pushed back the tears. "I don't know, okay? It's complicated."

"Well, try to explain then. Maybe you'll figure out why you made such a stupid decision."

This was so unfair. "I wanted to see the human world once in my thousands upon thousands of years that I would be living down here. I had to see it for myself sooner or later, Father, you knew that."

He shook his head. "No, no you didn't. I don't spend any time up there and I am perfectly happy down here."

"Stop lying to yourself Father, you are not happy down here. This job takes its toll on you and you damn wish you could rest like the other gods seem to everyday. You are stronger than them, yes, but you aren't that strong."

He didn't say a word but just stared at me.

I stood up. "You can't be mad at me forever. I don't deserve it, and neither do you. I messed up, okay? And I know that. But it could have been worse, and at least I get to spend time with you still, so you aren't alone. Now grow up and just learn how to forgive me."

After saying the last part, I didn't want to face him so I turned to the door to leave. Hades used his power to slam the door in front of my face before I could reach the hallway.

"Chrysanthemum…"

"I'm going to Maka's! And before you say anything, yes, I'm actually going there. At least she will listen to me."

He didn't re-open the door, so I used my power to get it out of my way. After the entire ordeal with Zeus, I had learned to control my powers a bit better. Although when I was furious, my powers still slipped somewhat beyond my control, but I could snap out of these flashes of anger with no help, especially since Huntley wasn't here to help calm my anger.

Storming out of the throne room, I realized I was acting a little like my mother. This made me a little more angry, especially since I didn't want to be anything like her. But I was pissed—I was pissed at my father, I was pissed at this situation, and more importantly I was pissed at myself.

I got back to my room and summoned a bag that I could put some clothes in. I didn't know how long I would stay at Maka's, also known as Makaria, my sort-of half sister who was created by my father, not born. He created her to deal with those who needed help leaving the earth to go to Asphodel Fields. Sometimes spirits refused and it was her duty to get them to leave the mortal world and find their way.

She was always busy with work, but I knew she would take time to listen. That was what she was good at, as she listened to every soul that didn't want to leave the mortal world. She had compassion and knew how to help those in needs. I was grateful to have her around, especially when this place sometimes felt so lonely.

I loved the Underworld and didn't want to leave to go to Olympus. The mortal world had been interesting, for sure, but it wasn't home. I had to find out, though, what it was like. It was only a matter of time and Father knew that.

Yet he wouldn't forgive me, and so far I knew he didn't forgive Persephone either. I didn't know how long this would last—especially since he was a god and had forever to hold a grudge. I wasn't patient like him, however, so he would have to get over it if he really wanted me to stay with him.

Throwing on the last pair of pants I would need for my trip, I zipped up my bag and headed to where Charon stayed. I would need him to get to Maka's safely. I would not make the same mistake twice.

Chapter 4

Huntley

It was cold still, even though we were past the winter solstice. It rained a lot in London, just like they always said in the movies. Since I had to move here, so to speak, it has been cold, wet, and foggy. I wasn't sure when the last time I had seen the sun was.

Though, according to myth, which I guess meant it was real now, the reason it was cold was because the mother of Persephone was weeping that her daughter was in the Underworld. Then when Persephone was back on the Earth, her mother rejoiced and spring and summer came. Talk about drama, though that would explain why Persephone was the way she was.

Although I hated the winter, I wasn't looking forward

to the summer either. When summer was here, that meant that we had even less time to figure out what to do to save Chrys. Or maybe by then, we will have figured something out. Ugh, I didn't want to think about it, yet I found myself thinking about it constantly. I never was one to keep my mind off of things, which was probably why I ended up in the Underworld to begin with. But as Pothos pointed out, it wouldn't be as simple to send myself to the Underworld, or to get Chrys out of there. I had no guarantee of being found, so we waited to figure something out.

One of the problems I had with walking around London was that it always reminded me of the time I spent with Chrys here. I felt like I was seeing her shadow constantly, that I should be able to turn around and find her there, smiling. She wasn't there though and I was stuck here permanently. Of course, this arrangement hopefully would only be temporary.

I headed towards the river. I spent a lot of time staring into the water, hoping in vain that she would just appear from nowhere with no forewarning. It wasn't ever the case, but it gave me something to do. I also liked the water in general, as I thought the element was beautiful. I mean, the River Thames wasn't the best thing to look at as it was quite brown and polluted, but the idea was there.

I kept my head down, not wanting to look at any of the pedestrians that crowded the streets. There was always a girl that looked sort of like Chrys and made my heart race for a moment. But then I find out she's just a stranger and I become lonely once again.

Keeping one's head down also made it so people didn't bother you, or at least usually. There were always those people that felt entitled to have anyone help them, even if it would bother the stranger. Those types of people didn't like my comments, and I either heard them yelling at me from a block away or could feel their eyes glaring at me until I rounded a corner. Either way, it was so worth it.

I took a deep breath of the crisp, wet air, wondering who I should pray to for this to all get sorted out. It wasn't like I could pray to the God of Gods since he was the problem to begin with. No, I prayed to the hope I had, and determination to figure this all out. Then maybe Chrys will be safe.

I still wasn't sure how we would do it. The only idea I had was to hide Chrys, but where? Zeus was the Gods of Gods and could find us no matter what. The only reason Hades and Persephone could hide her was because Zeus didn't know she existed. Now he knew and would stop at nothing to have her. It was ridiculous how much he feared her. I mean, I knew she was powerful, especially considering how easily she took out Poseidon, which still made me laugh thinking about it. He thought he was so powerful because he was a God of Olympus, only to be outdone by a girl that was the daughter of Hades and Persephone.

I thought about that night often—the night she was taken away. She was still so naïve when it came to using her powers and didn't even remember when the rage kicked in. Her anger is what would bring it up from deep within her, and when Poseidon tried to kidnap her, it was the last thing needed to completely trigger her powers. She could bring instant death and life to anything she wanted, which was exactly why Zeus feared her. He didn't believe any god should be so powerful, even if Chrys could control her powers. Then he tried to kill her.

Scratching my face, I thought back at how Hades had shown up. Zeus, his own brother, didn't think Hades would show up for his daughter. How did Hades even know where we were? I guess I would never understand how these gods worked.

Hades had looked so disappointed in Chrys, I had never seen him so mad at her. They almost never fought, unlike Hades and Persephone who fought all the time. Their relationship kind of reminded me of my own parents, although a lot tamer in contrast, which was saying a lot. I couldn't count the times I hid in my room while my parents screamed at each other.

However, mortal fights were not the same as god fights. They could hold grudges, hurt each other unlike any human could, it was crazy. I just hoped that I would never have to face Hades' wrath.

Sighing, I ventured over towards South Kensington. I debated if I wanted to take the Underground, but figured it would be easier to walk. Anytime I went into the Underground, I found that I usually pissed off a worker one way or another. I never meant to do it on purpose, but somehow I always managed to do it. I would just take the Underground on the way back since it would be dark by then. I didn't need people to think I was some kind of thug they could beat up... again.

I swore that Zeus sent mortals to pick a fight with me, just to see what I would do. I had gotten into at least ten fist fights now, and a few knife fights, in the last three months. And I didn't start it, which Pothos never believed. But I didn't and I swore there was something wrong with those thugs. They seemed almost zombie-like, and it only happened at night.

It wasn't anything I couldn't deal with, though, and so far so good, but I tried not to go out at night anymore, just in case.

As I rounded the corner, I noticed someone I recognized even though I was looking down at the ground as I walked. It could have been her demeanor, or the fact she was one of the few people I saw for a few years. Either way, I found Persephone standing in front of me. She had on a long tan coat with tights and high-heeled boots. I wasn't sure how she wasn't cold, but either way, it was what she was wearing. Next to her was another female, who appeared a little older than her with long blonde hair, a high-and-mighty nose, and was wearing pretty much the same thing as Persephone, except her jacket was blue.

I should have just ignored Persephone, but by the time everything registered through my head, I was beginning to see red.

"You have some nerve showing your face in this city after what happened!" I yelled out at her. I was surprised at myself after I said the words out loud. Was I really going to just talk to a goddess like this? Guess I was.

She either didn't think I would simply start yelling at her or she hadn't recognized me until that point. The other woman's face looked as if it were in shock. I guess she never imagined that I would just start yelling. I didn't care what she thought—if she was hanging around Persephone, then she probably wasn't the best sort of person either.

"Huntley, this isn't the place," Persephone began as she glanced around. People were staring at us now, wondering why some kid like me would be yelling at some beautiful women. I could tell some men were about to act if I did anything rash, which I wouldn't. I wasn't that kind of guy.

"You think I care?" I asked. "You think after what you did to Chrys that I would just stand by and watch?"

"Huntley!" She demanded. People started to ignore us and go about their day. I think the moment they heard me say a person's name that it was some petty argument, although this was anything but petty.

"Persephone," the blonde woman next to her placed her hand on Persephone's shoulder. "Don't bother yourself with this human. He clearly doesn't understand our way of life. Besides, he sort of reminds me of your husband, and I want nothing to do with someone like that."

This woman clearly was another goddess, especially with the comment about Hades, but I wasn't sure which one. She couldn't have been that great if she disliked him since he was the kindest person I had ever met, god or not. I didn't really care at this moment either, all I cared about was letting Persephone have it.

She tried to walk away, her friend grabbing her arm to move, but I quickly blocked them.

"You pushed Chrys over the edge and you don't even care that she is going to marry Zeus in a few months."

Now people began staring again. They probably heard the word "Zeus" and thought I was crazy, or that some weird parents named their kid Zeus. Either way, I had captured their attention. I was so glad I could be of some entertainment for people.

Persephone shook her head. "That has nothing to do with me, she was the one who—"

"Are you kidding me? You come home for three months the year and all you do is talk about Earth, sneak in humans to fuck, and then think you aren't to blame?! You disgust me."

"Hey!" the woman next to Persephone stepped in front of her. Her face was red and she looked like one of those girls who would take their rings off before stabbing you in the stomach and watching you bleed. Maybe she wasn't the best person to have this conversation with in front of Persephone.

She went on, "you have no right to talk to my daughter like that, especially as a human. We could destroy you in a matter of seconds if you keep this up!"

So she was Persephone's mother, Demeter. It was interesting how at a certain point everyone almost looked the same age, even though they could be thousands of years older than the other. This definitely explained the stuck-up nose she had.

"Mother, don't worry about it, all right? He is just love-struck with my daughter." She turned back to me. "Huntley, I can't undo the past, okay? Just move on. There is nothing we can do."

I shook my head. "I can't believe you would say that about your own daughter. And your granddaughter. Tell me, do you even care about her? Have any feelings of love or sympathy toward her? Or are you just so self-absorbed that you are about nothing except your own desire and greed?"

Demeter looked like she wanted to kill me, but Persephone put her hand in front of her.

"Huntley…" Persephone began, but I turned around.

"I'm done with you. I don't want to see your face again. I will go save Chrys if it's the last thing I do, because I actually care about her. Just stay out of my way."

With that, I walked away. I didn't want to hear any more, and I doubted she really wanted to explain herself to me. I didn't understand these gods and how selfish they could be. You would think after so many years that they would learn how to be more caring. Apparently it was just the opposite.

I just hoped that when I lived for that long, I wouldn't turn into one of them.

Chapter 5

Chrys

I didn't want to be fighting with my father when time was running out for me, but he was being a real dick lately. I needed someone to talk to, especially since I had absolutely no one to talk to in the palace any longer, or at least not anyone who I can confide in as a trusted friend. I could talk to Cerberus, but he would just look at me with one or more of his heads slightly crooked and concerned. It was absolutely dead in the palace, with only Hades and I living here, excluding staff and the Three Stooges. I didn't talk to any of them that often, as the staff changed quite often, and the Three Stooges were, well, lacking of any personality that wasn't selfishness.

So that was why I was on my way to Maka's.

Maka's place was far away, or at least within the Underworld. I had to have Charon take me this time, for a couple of reasons. First off, Father insisted if I travel anywhere, then Charon had to guide me. Second, I really didn't want to try to navigate the rivers again since I was alone this time, although A.J. and Huntley weren't that much help. But I still didn't want to try to get there on my own. Almost drowning once wasn't that fun.

Charon was an interesting fellow for sure. I think because he was so lonely from traveling through the rivers for who knew how long that he started to go a little insane. Especially since most people weren't buried with a coin anymore to tip him with. It made him feel unappreciated, even though he didn't need the money. To be honest, I didn't even know what he did with it. But, worst of all, he was a talker. He talked, a lot, about random things that he thought were funny when they really weren't. It was frustrating sometimes, so I learned how to tune him out. Father was a pro at it.

"So Chrys, have I told you the story of when your father first started this business?" he began.

I didn't even try to reply. The answer was yes, he had. Every year for the past several hundred years. He repeated stories so often that A.J., Huntley, and I began calling each other "Charon" if we repeated a story.

"He was given this place after Zeus saved everyone from their father, Kronos, and sent him to Tartarus, where a lot of the old titans and the creatures before the titans were sent. It was a crazy time back then, or at least so I hear. *I'm* not that old." He laughed at his own joke. It wasn't that funny, especially since I've heard it a million times already. "I'm not nearly as old as most of the Olympic gods. No, they are old grandpas compared to me."

I took in a deep breath and let it out slowly. I couldn't wait until this ride was over. It also made it so I wouldn't want to leave Maka's, in fear of having to hear the same story once more. I tried to distract myself by looking around. The different rivers that spanned out in all directions from the palace were shining a beautiful sapphire blue. I watched as they glistened in the light that came from the ocean that encased the entire Underworld. It was nothing like the sky in the mortal world but more like being underneath ocean waves, looking up at the hot glowing sun. I found it a lot more beautiful than the mortal world.

As for the rest of the Underworld, near the palace was Tartarus, a large rainfall of souls getting sucked into eternal torment. It was where my grandfather was trapped, just as Charon had said. I knew he was a horrible titan, but that was about it. It was rather strange to think I was related to such a monster, but then again, relations in the god world meant nothing in the end.

On the other side of the palace were Asphodel Meadows and Elysian Fields, for humans and gods respectively. Not many gods died that often, and demigods seemed to only die every once in a while, as many gods stopped fraternizing with humans in the past few centuries due to their destructive power. Not many trusted humans anymore, or if they did want to have sex with them, they used some kind of condom. At least, that was what I concluded.

Charon apparently was still telling his story. "Anyway, Zeus didn't trust your dad so that's when he sent the three judges to help. Zeus definitely has trust issues. They are probably daddy issues since he had to kill his dad and send him to Tartarus. Then he goes behind his wife's back and humps anything that moves. So I guess he doesn't trust himself since he's a big liar"

I didn't want to hear Zeus' name at the moment, as I didn't want to be reminded of what was awaiting me. And I agreed. He did definitely want to hump anything that moved. Myself included. I shuddered at the thought. It was a subject that Father and I didn't want to discuss.

"Although his wife is also a piece of work. She is really possessive and scary as hell, well I guess scarier since we are in hell and it ain't that bad here. So I guess scarier... than Tartarus. Well that isn't true, nothing is scarier than that place."

I let out yet another impatient breath. He wouldn't notice, he was pretty clueless. I wondered how many souls have thought about jumping off this boat while hearing him talk. They probably didn't even care and were in shock that they had died. I know I would be.

I wondered what happened when one of the gods of the Underworld died, like me or Charon. Did we just get stuck in one of the three afterlives, or did nothing happen? I know Zeus could have sent me to Tartarus, as he and my father were the only ones who could do that, but what if I was destroyed by something else?

It was a subject that I had never brought up with my father, mainly because I didn't want to know the answer to it. I had this fear that if I died, I would go straight to Tartarus, especially since I was never supposed to be born. I could travel to Asphodel Fields and Elysian Meadows without any trouble and leave whenever I wanted, but Tartarus was another story. If I fell into it, if I just happened to travel inside the never-ending waterfall of fear and death, I would drown forever.

Charon was right—it was the scariest thing out there.

"She's what the young kids call a 'yandere'." He smiled as if that bit of knowledge was supposed to impress me. "I learned that term a couple weeks ago. It's what all the cool kids call an obsessive girl who murders for her love. It's cray-cray."

I rolled my eyes. He always thought he was up to par with the new terms. I didn't care about that sort of thing, especially since they were fleeting compared to us.

"Now where was I? Oh yes, Hera. She's scary, if I were you I would try to stay away from her, especially when it comes to Zeus."

And here I thought he stayed up with the latest gossip. Well, if no one told him about my engagement with Zeus, I wasn't going to tell him. I didn't want to hear the things he would comment on.

"She has destroyed many women's lives, then again it was really Zeus who destroyed their lives if you really look at it. For someone who doesn't want shit to happen, he sure brings chaos to many people. Your father though, he doesn't bring chaos to anyone. He brings them fairness, and delivers what they deserve, yet he is treated by humans to be the worse one of them all. How weird is that?"

I wanted this ride to be over so badly. So. Very. Badly.

It never occurred to me that I would have to face Hera. I mean, she had to have known about the engagement already, right? Was she mad? Was she going to make my life a living hell, not that it wasn't already? I didn't even want to think about it. I was traveling to Maka to forget about my problems, not to worry about more. Damn Charon and his endless talking.

"So are you going to take over for him after he retires, that is, if he ever retires. Can a god retire , I wonder? I sure want to retire. No one appreciates me these days. No one has a token for me or anything. How do they think I pay the rent?" He laughed. "That's a joke, I don't pay rent. Your dad never makes us pay rent. For real, I guess I don't need the tips, except for getting some cool clothes. Got to stay up with the fashion, you know."

So he spent his money on clothes? I actually kind of wanted to see that. Right now he was wearing a long black cloak, just as he always was. I never had seen what he wore underneath, and I had a fear for the longest time that he was in fact not wearing anything. That was why I never asked. As for what he wears outside of work… it had to be something really ridiculous, I couldn't even imagine.

As I glanced up, I could see Maka's place. Thank the gods, I wanted to get off of this boat so badly.

Maka's home was rather... unique, to say the least. It was like something out of a fairy tale, but not the good kind. She spent a lot of time with Hekate, whom witches liked learning from. This place was like an old witch's hovel, with a strange fog hiding it from any passerby's glance. It looked like it was made of old wood and straw, Smoke was coming out of the fireplace. The candles in the windows flickered, beckoning anyone to come near.

I loved it here.

"I also enjoy having some wonderful meals, which cost some money as well—that is if I could get away. Usually just make frozen meals these days. The other day..."

"Charon," I said. He didn't hear me, as usual.

"... superb mac and cheese and..."

"Charon!" I yelled this time.

He turned to me. "What is it?"

"We are here."

He turned to face the dock with a bit of a frown. "Oh, I guess we are. Well have a pleasant visit and don't forget to leave a review on 'charon gondola dot com'." He laughed at his own joke again.

I grabbed my backpack the moment the boat got near the dock and jumped off. "Thanks Charon, see you later."

"Until then, see ya' Chrys."

He sailed off, heading back to port to pick up the dead and carry them to their destination. I turned towards Maka's house, which still made me smile on how witchy it was. Deciding to fit in, I snapped my fingers and changed my clothes into a modern, medieval-inspired outfit. This outfit comprised a white, off-the-shoulders blouse, a black tunic, a silver belt at the waist, and a two-layered purple skirt with black boots. I felt fantastic in it, and a bit like a witch too. And yeah, I didn't really need to pack since I had powers, but that was beside the point. But it is a great stress reliever to angrily pack a suitcase.

Now, time to go talk to Maka and see if she has any solutions for my problems.

Chapter 6

Huntley

I needed to find something that would help me relax, but I had no idea what would help. When I was younger, I would always turn to drugs. Meth, marijuana, LSD—you name it, I've probably tried it. I was so glad that this new body didn't have any of the withdrawal symptoms like I had before I died, although I had died for it to happen, so there was that. All that was the old me though, and the new me wanted nothing to do with that type of life.

However, now I found myself without an outlet. I was never taught how to have a healthy outlet. Between my so-called friends and parents, all I had was drugs, alcohol, and violence, and now I was stuck just panicking constantly. I debated on what to do, who to turn to, but I didn't have anyone close to me other than Pothos and Mel. And Prometheus, I presumed, if he ever reappeared.

I didn't want to turn to them for this problem, mainly because I felt very human complaining about something little. I wanted them to focus more on Chrys and how to help her rather than some stupid mental thing I couldn't get over. I also didn't believe they knew anything that could help me, so I never brought it up. I needed a distraction, but as to what could really distract me, I knew of nothing. Movies, food, games, none of it helped. I couldn't stop worrying.

Was Chrys feeling the same thing? Did she really miss me?

I knew the answer was yes, or at least to the last question. Her worries were probably a little different since she was the one facing the true problem: having to marry Zeus. I felt so helpless, for both of us. I knew she couldn't do anything on her side, not when Zeus now knew exactly where to find her.

I wondered what Hades would do to stop this wedding. If I knew him, which I believed that I did, he would figure something out, as well, to help her. I just wished there was a way I could talk to him—to figure out a way to help.

Especially since his wife was doing nothing.

Running into Persephone made my blood pump even more. I was still so furious at her I was lucky I didn't try to throw a punch her way. I didn't care if she was a girl; she was a goddess after all. It probably wouldn't have even hurt given her superior strength.

But then there was Demeter. She wouldn't have been too happy if I had punched her daughter. She probably would have used some kind of godly power to destroy me, or curse me, or something far more powerful. Either way, it would have sucked.

Persephone definitely didn't fall far from the tree. No wonder she was so stuck up with a mother like that. I felt pretty bad for Hades having to deal with a mother-in-law like that. And his Father-in-Law was Zeus. And brother. And now…

Nope, not going to think about it. I had to tell myself that on a daily basis. Gods and goddesses were not like humans. Repeat, gods and goddesses were not like humans. Their family relationships weren't the same. Their blood is not the same. It had been months, years if you counted my time in the Underworld, where I had learned about the "relationships". I couldn't wrap my mind around it and tried my hardest to ignore it. But, even if I tried to ignore it, I knew deep down that the gods were into some weird shit. Weird southern shit.

I didn't know where exactly I was heading. Earlier I had been heading towards Kensington but now I was going aimlessly about the city, hoping for an idea of some sort, and to walk off my earlier argument with Persephone. I hated this helpless feeling I was having and hoped that Prometheus would be back soon so we could start to actually do something. Anything, really, other than just standing around doing nothing.

Or wandering around London, doing nothing.

As I rounded yet another street corner, I found myself standing in front of the entrance to Hyde Park, where the preacher box lay. Sometimes I liked to hear people talk on it, just to see what they would say. A lot of the time it was someone spouting complete bullshit, and I enjoyed hearing how stupid people were. Well, not really because it meant this world was pathetic and going to crumble probably, but on the bright side, I knew what happened after everyone died.

Today a man stood carrying with him a sign saying that war will never equal peace. People were yelling at him, calling him a hippie, saying that he didn't understand reality, but the man didn't flinch. He stayed still, his eyes looked sad at the world around him and he kept his bearded mouth shut. His curly white hair matched his aging skin and worn-out clothes. He actually did kind of look like a hippie, but in this case, it seemed he was protesting out of weariness with the world than out of belief.

I glanced around at the people shouting at him. They seemed to be just there to argue out of rage rather than actual belief. It was interesting to say the least to watch them respond to someone so non-threatening. There was so much anger in everyone, myself included, and many took it out on what or who they saw was weak.

A suited gentleman next to me scoffed at the man. I looked over at him to see his face covered in disdain. He was rather clean-shaven, his hair looking like every other suited man over forty.

He whispered, "People don't realize how important

war is, and what I have sacrificed to rule it."

I whipped back around, not wanting him to notice me. Shit, did he say rule? As in god of war? Was he Ares?

Probably not someone whose attention I wanted to receive.

Wanting to get away as fast as I could, I hurried off into the park. I doubted he would know it was me, if anyone even knew who I was. I mainly had a fear that Zeus wanted me to suffer and told all the gods I was some kind of evil being they needed to stop, especially since he probably knew I was doing my best to stop the wedding. Better safe than sorry.

I shook my head. What, do all the gods just hang out around London? Is this the happening place? The more I thought about it, the more I wondered if it was because of Chrys, that the gods loitering around London were sent here by Zeus to make sure we weren't planning something to foil his plans. Even if that wasn't the case, I knew I had to keep a look out, as did Prometheus, Pothos, and Mel.

That was why we had to move slowly in order to help Chrys, or at least what Pothos said. He didn't want to raise any alarms that could make Zeus come down here and wipe us off the planet, or worse. I didn't know what the "or worse" was, but the fact that all the gods said that when they talked about Zeus didn't make me feel better about Chrys going to marry him. And then there were the stories about Hera I heard…

Although it was still cold out, the park was beautiful and refreshing compared to the bustling city. Don't get me wrong, London is rather beautiful in its buildings, but something about the forest made me calm down instantly.

Even though it was winter, there were still a lot of tourists around, probably due to lower travel costs during off-peak times. I was starting to get really sick of all the tourist and could understand how natives to the area seemed rude to them. Tourists were obnoxious, thinking the city was all for them and they could do whatever they want. They didn't realize that this was still an active, thriving city. And tourists always just got in the way of that.

I did, however, figure out the best spots in Hyde Park that didn't have many people. It was deep within the park where no one wanted to walk all the way into, mainly because they thought thugs hung out there. The answer to that was no, just me, although to most I just looked like a punk. I didn't care what anyone thought of me, though, and figured it was none of their business, anyway. There was only one person's opinion I cared about, and that was Chrys', and she never judged me for the life I lived, even though it was technically her job.

I found my little hideaway, a dark area where the trees were the thickest near the middle of the park. It was quiet, not even a bird making a noise here. I leaned against the tree and tried to let all the anger leave my body. It was serene here, almost magical. It was a feeling I wish I could share with Chrys.

If only Chrys were here with me.

That was my problem, I kept thinking about her and it

made me even more miserable. I felt obsessed but it wasn't necessarily because I wanted her around constantly, but more I didn't want her to suffer like she will once she married Zeus. Especially after hearing all the stories about Zeus from Pothos and Mel. He sounded like a monster, even more so than his father Kronos. Well, that I wasn't sure of. Kronos had eaten his children and all. Then there was a war of the gods against the titans, of which I still wasn't quite sure how I felt about Prometheus' role in that. He had betrayed the rest of the titans to side with the gods, whom he knew would win. Did that mean he always took the easy way out? I guess that wasn't true since he helped humans gain fire and knowledge. I just had to wait and see, something I wasn't very good at, especially since I didn't trust him as far as I could throw him. Pothos seemed to trust him, though, and I trusted Pothos now. It took a while, I had to admit, but after they went through all the trouble with trying to return Chrys to the Underworld, I knew they were honest enough. They were brazen enough to want to stand up against Zeus.

Taking in a deep breath, I let my thoughts try to leave Chrys and be present of where I was at. The crisp air filled my lungs and I tried to ground myself with the tree that I leaned against. There was something to be said about trees and how they could make you feel grounded. I never believed it when people talked about it, but after sitting here for a while, I noticed a bit of a difference. However, the moment would pass when I left the tree, leaving me still frustrated. I needed to find another outlet, but at least I could have a couple moments of peace.

Sliding my back down the tree into a sitting position, I closed my eyes and let the feeling take me away.

Chapter 7

Chrys

I didn't even have to knock on Maka's door as she swung it open the moment I arrived.

"Chrysanthemum!"

She about knocked me over as she wrapped her arms around me. Finally, after a long time, I was feeling someone's embrace. I had spent so many nights cold and alone, crying myself asleep. This was exactly what I needed. To spend some quality "goddess" time, after having to be cooped up with a bunch of dudes for so long. Her body was warm against mine and it felt refreshing. I craved the company of others more than my father, I knew, but I never knew how to tell anyone that.

She backed up, her hands coming forward to grab my

own. "It's been so long, Chrysanthemum, how have you been?"

Even though I was excited to see her, I couldn't stand her calling me by my full name. Something about it just made me cringe. "Maka, how many times have I told you to call me Chrys?"

She raised an eyebrow at me, which was her signature look. "I have known you since you were a baby. I can call you whatever I want."

I rolled my eyes. That was always her answer. I didn't know why I even bothered. "Whatever. It's just nice to get away."

She examined me for a moment and must have noticed the sadness in my eyes. "What's wrong?"

Did she not know about what happened in the mortal world? She was busy with work a lot, and was kind of outside of the realm of the gods, so to speak. She didn't talk to many gods, only those in the Underworld. If Charon didn't know yet, maybe she didn't either.

I opened my mouth, but I didn't even know where to begin. So much had happened.

She knew what I was thinking and pulled me through the entry. "Well, come on in and I will start us a pot of tea."

Following her, I was welcomed with the smell of warm incense. It was earthy and sweet and it always made me calm. I always wanted to take some home with me, but learned long ago that Father hated the smell. I was totally bringing some back with me this time, whether he liked it or not. The castle was enormous, he could get over it by just going to the other side of the castle.

Maka would never tell me what was in the recipe, but called it "Vampire's Blood." The name was intriguing enough, and I swore there had to be some kinds of resins in it. Maybe she would teach me how to make it someday.

The inside was decorated like a combination of the potion and herbology classrooms from Hogwarts. There were different dried plants everywhere that Maka had grabbed from Earth. She was the Goddess of Blessed Death and had all of this stuff to help those who had died along the path to the afterlife. She was nice, but if you got on her bad side, then she was a power to reckon with. I had heard stories from Father that left me wondering if we were talking about the same person.

In addition to the herbs, there were bottles lining the shelves throughout the main room. To the right was the kitchen, full of even more herbs and potions, and up the stairs were two separate bedrooms—one for her and one for guests, which was mainly me.

I took a seat while Maka went into the kitchen to make some tea. I glanced around, admiring the old paintings that hadn't changed in centuries. They were all oil paintings she did herself, the dark greens and purples, mixed together in a lovely duet. Each painting was of a different plant, and how that plant was tied to death. Many mortals saw death as a horrible thing which I could understand, however when you lived in the land of death, you learned to see the beauty that surrounded it. It was one of my favorite things to see at Maka's.

A few minutes later, Maka came in with a tray of tea and treats. The tea was a beautiful red color and the plate of shortbread looked delicious. Maka made the best shortbread. Not even Father's cooks could come close to how amazing these were.

Maka set the dish down and sat across from me. Pouring the tea into matching green and white porcelain cups, she began, "so, are you going to tell me what is bothering you or do I have to take a wild guess?"

I grabbed the cup of tea and let it warm my hands. "Is it a wild guess? Although I know news doesn't travel to you quite that fast, I have a feeling you've been acting naïve on purpose."

She nodded as she grabbed a piece of shortbread. "You mean, do I know that you snuck out of the Underworld to go to Earth, using me as a scapegoat might I add, and then got caught by Zeus? Hades then tried to save you but wasn't completely successful. In the end, you had to promise to marry Zeus and sent Huntley back to be stuck on Earth as Zeus was afraid he might ruin his plans. Does that pretty much sum it up?"

So she had heard. Well, I guess that meant I didn't have to feel the shame of telling her myself. I winced and slowly nodded. "Pretty much."

Maka sighed as she took a bite of the shortbread. Little crumbs fell off and landed on her dress. She was always a messy eater. "You do realize that your father came here first to look for you. You should have seen his face—he was worried sick. I've never seen him look so scared in my life."

"Yeah, well, he doesn't really seem to care anymore," I murmured into my teacup as I took a drink. The tea was rather tart in taste, but I could feel instantly how it warmed me up and made my chest feel less heavy. "Wow, this tea is amazing. What's in it?"

"This is actually a formula I made long ago when your parents first got together. I designed it for your mother when she was torn between her mother and Hades. This helped her straighten herself out."

Ugh, great. I did not want to think of her at that moment. "Yeah, and she decided that the Underworld is a horrible place and being with Demeter is a lot better."

Maka shook her head. "That wasn't always the case. Your father and mother were once madly in love, but it caused a lot of drama in Olympus. Over the centuries, the stress got to your mother and now she acts the way she does."

I had never heard that story. It still didn't mean I forgave her for how she treated Father and I, but I wondered what the other gods did to make her change her mind on just how much she loved Father.

"But you asked what was in it," Maka continued. "It has chamomile, hibiscus, rose petals, rose hips, and damiana. But in this batch, I added a little chrysanthemum because I couldn't help myself."

I laughed. She liked to add chrysanthemums to anything she made for me because she found it ironic. Luckily, I loved the taste of the flower. "Well, the tea is fantastic. It has made me feel a little better already."

"It helps the feelings settle, yes, but it doesn't make the

problem go away. Remember that."

That I understood. So much had happened in the last few months and I knew no matter what I took, it wouldn't make it go away. I had to face it myself. "Yeah, I know."

"So, tell me, why are you here? It's been quite a few weeks since everything happened. Why have you come to visit me now?"

I took another sip of the tea. "I don't know, I guess I just have had it with arguing with Father. He and I aren't really on speaking terms and when we do talk we just start fighting."

"I see," she took another bite and brushed off the crumbs. "He's being stubborn then."

Stubborn was another word for it. I leaned back in the cushy armchair and went on. "He thinks I've betrayed him somehow and have destroyed everything. He doesn't want me marrying Zeus and doesn't even want to look at me right now."

"That's a god for you, never able to rationalize their emotions. He's just scared his baby will get hurt."

"I can take care of myself, he needs to realize that. I couldn't stay stuck here forever."

"I know that, and he probably does too. He's just not happy about it. Give him some time and he will come around."

I set the cup down and grabbed a piece of shortbread. I took a big bite, the sweetness filling my mouth. These always hit the spot. If I could, I would eat a whole big plate full.

Thinking back to Father, I truly wondered if he would ever come around. He was pissed and blamed everyone he could, myself included. It was the only way he could cope, apparently, and I didn't see an end to it.

"I don't know that he will. He's really furious with me. I just don't know what to do, I'm so alone in that palace right now."

Maka leaned forwards and stared me straight in the eyes—those eyes that could pierce one's soul. I swore she could see everything when she looked at me like that. "What do you want?" She let the words linger. I didn't have an answer for her. "Honestly, Chrysanthemum, if you could have your way, what would you want?"

"I guess..." I took a deep breath and let the words come out of my mouth. "I guess I would want to find a way to get out of the marriage with Zeus, to see Huntley again, and to stay here in the Underworld with Father."

"Then make it happen," Maka stated, as if it was no big deal. She always saw the world like that—as if anything was possible if you put your mind to it. I wonder if that was the same advice she had given my mother. Look how that turned out...

I shook my head, "it isn't possible, Zeus always gets his way. There would be no way for me to get out of this wedding." Having heard all the stories about Zeus, I knew that to be reality. Zeus always got his way and he let nothing deter him. So many stories popped up in my head and none of them ended with Zeus retreating. Well, unless maybe when Hera was involved.

"Well," Maka began. "You already know that Huntley

is working hard to find a way to get you out of this, and there are probably things you could do as well."

"Oh yeah?" I asked. "Like what? I'm a little trapped at the moment. There isn't much I can do in the Underworld, that's why Father thought it was a great hiding place, and then I ruined that so there is nothing left."

She gave a little sly smile. "There is one thing left—at least that I know of. The Fates."

I wrinkled my nose. The Fates were... peculiar, for lack of a better word. Three old hags, all sisters, who sat around and bickered at each other about what they saw in people's future. They each saw a different part of one's life, and even though they knew that, they still argued about what that person would go through. I didn't want to visit them. Like I really didn't want to. On top of having to hear their loud shrieking voices, their place smelled like mothballs and mold. It was nasty.

Maka frowned. "Don't give me that face, you know that once you get them to actually talk about what you want, they speak the truth."

I let out a breath. "Fine, but I have to point out that between them and Charon, it's a wonder not everyone in the Underworld is crazy."

Maka shrugged. "That's to be decided . But I am serious. What do you say about going tomorrow?"

I thought about it for a moment, then reluctantly nodded. "Fine. Not like it will hurt anything."

Chapter 8

<u>Huntley</u>

After all this time wandering the streets of London, wondering when Prometheus would return, I opened the door to the flat to find the bastard standing in front of me.

Prometheus was back.

"You!" It was the only word I could think of. I felt stupid for just pointing at him, flabbergasted, not being able to put words together.

He gave me a funny look. "Yes, it is me. Very human of you to point that out."

I clenched my fist. No, I wouldn't punch him. Not until I heard what he had to say about saving Chrys first. Then maybe.

"What did you figure out? What did you find?" I asked anxiously as I followed him into the living room.

He collapsed on the couch and pinched the bridge of his nose. "Not until Pothos and Mel get back. I want everyone here.

"Are you kidding me? You've taken months to search for something and you are going to have me wait longer?"

Prometheus let out a deep breath. "You've waited months, therefore you can wait a few more minutes, maybe an hour."

He had a point, but I didn't want to admit that. I just wanted to figure something out now and save Chrys. Energy was pumping through my entire body and I couldn't keep still. Why were these gods so relaxed about this entire situation? Didn't they understand an innocent girl's life was at stake?

Since Prometheus wasn't talking, and I didn't feel like making small talk, I decided to just stand against the wall and thump my head against it.

Thump. Thump. Thump. Thump.

"Could you not be an annoying human for a change?" Prometheus asked. He was still just sitting on the couch, calm, almost like nothing was wrong.

"I don't know, could you not be an asshole of a god for a change?" I shouldn't have said that, I knew, but he was really getting on my nerves.

"I have gone out of my way for you—even risked my life, and you are going to bite my head off?"

He had a point. "Sorry. but I'm not going to stop

hitting my head against the wall."

Prometheus shook his head. "You are a stupid human, I don't understand why I ever thought your kind was worth millennia of agony."

"Which also makes me wonder why you are helping us in the first place, if you are so scared of Zeus."

Prometheus held my gaze. "As I said before, I want to trick Zeus but not in a way that we would get caught. This would be more like cheating at poker without getting caught."

I still wasn't sure what his angle was, I supposed he just wanted to help Hades out. Poor Hades always got screwed over. But I still didn't quite believe that. There had to be an ulterior motive, but as to what that was, I wasn't sure.

"Yet for some reason, I don't believe you."

He shook his head. "Whatever."

Thump. Thump. Thump.

It was a good hour before Pothos and Mel were back with a couple sacks of groceries. Oh that was right. They told me this morning that they were going to stop by the store. I had forgotten. I felt a bit like a dick since I promised to go with them, then didn't come back from my walk in time. I would have remembered if I hadn't run into Persephone. That was a lie, I probably wouldn't have remembered either way.

"Huntley, what did I say about hitting your head on the wall?" Pothos said the moment he saw me.

"To not to?" I asked.

He let out a sigh—something all the gods seemed to

like to do. It was like I was an untrained dog that they couldn't get to obey. Every time they did it, it made me a little more frustrated. I wasn't just some measly human that they could keep treating this way.

"Prometheus, you had me worried to death! I missed you baby!" She jumped into his arms and kissed him on the cheek. He didn't reveal any emotion on his face, but kept his stern look about him. I wondered how he really felt about Mel. I mean, he left her here and has tried to run away from her a few times now. He probably just doesn't want to piss her off due to her being the Goddess of Ghosts.

"Did you really have to drop everything? You had the eggs in your bag!" Pothos called over. "I swear to Zeus if you got egg on my carpet, I will send you to Tartarus myself!"

I helped him pick up the stuff out of the bag. Luckily the eggs didn't break. Quickly placing everything in the kitchen, we went into the living room to see what Prometheus had to say.

Mel was still in Prometheus' lap, sitting across him, playing with his hair as he ignored her and began talking to Pothos and I. "I had to travel far to find what I was looking for, but I think I found a way to help Chrys."

"And that is?" I asked with a little sarcasm in my voice. I didn't mean to have it come out that way, but as always, it did.

Prometheus gave me a look and then went on. "As I had said earlier, I was one of the few that tricked Zeus and didn't get killed. I did get tortured, but I learned my lesson on how to not get caught. There are a few other gods that could be helpful as well, one in particular who would know how to stay out of Zeus' sight. He, however, has been hiding for many years and I wasn't even sure where to find him. I asked around, going wherever I was led. I first talked to Artemis, who was deep in the woods of Germany. She then led me to Apollo, who in turn led me to Aphrodite, but that took a little... persuasion for her to tell me anything."

"That bitch," Mel whispered.

I rolled my eyes. Of course, she would get jealous of Aphrodite. "Get to the point, who were you looking for?"

"I'm telling you why it took so long since you seem so impatient. It takes a while to find a god if he is hiding, especially when you can't ask the one person who can see all the gods, aka Zeus. Anyway, I was saying, all these gods ended up leading me back to the UK. The god I was looking for was here all along. I was going to go talk to him before reporting back, but I figured it would be better if we all went to hear what he had to say."

"Again," I tried to calm myself down. "Who are we talking to?"

"Dionysus. He would be able to tell us how to get Chrys out of this marriage."

Pothos perked up. "You found him? Many of the gods have been looking for him for years."

Could a god really hide that well? I mean, I knew humans could escape and hide from others for a long period of time, even until they die, but it seemed like a god would have a harder time, unless they were in the Underworld of course. I mean, Chrys had only been on the Earth for a couple of days before someone found her, although A.J. was the reason for that. He had alerted his father, Poseidon, of our whereabouts and once Chrys was threatened, her power was like a big radar, alerting everyone to her presence. It was quite the show though.

Prometheus nodded. "Yes. And he will have the knowledge we need. Many gods had only heard rumors, however Aphrodite seems to keep tabs on him. And don't worry, no one knows why I was looking for him, nor do they care, but as a safety measure, none of them remember talking with me and won't be reporting to Zeus of my whereabouts."

"How did you manage that?" I asked.

Prometheus held up a small blue bottle. It reminded me of the rivers in the Underworld—a pure blue color. "Got this from a little black birdie before he left to go back to the Underworld. I guess he knew what he needed to do."

I read the inscription. "Lethe? What's that?"

Pothos gasped. "Did Hades give that to you when he was here? He must have had it ready to use when he was looking for Chrys. Then when he found Zeus, he knew that it wouldn't work on him. Damn, smart man."

"What am I missing?" I asked.

Pothos turned to me. "That is water from the river Lethe, also known as the river of unmindfulness. Anyone who drinks that will forget everything that happened within a certain time frame, depending on the amount used. A drop would take away a couple of hours."

Prometheus nodded. "And that was exactly what it did. It was fascinating, actually, to watch. I never thought I would ever see it in action, at least not without forgetting it. Hades has never given out any of the Underground specialties before. He must really care for his daughter."

"That he does," Mel said. "If he was willing to oppose Zeus the way he did. I've never seen him stand up to him like that before."

We were silent for a moment, thinking back to when he stood in front of Zeus and absorbed the power of his lightning, which I didn't even understand how that was possible. Zeus had meant to kill Chrys and send her to Tartarus, so how would Hades be able to stop that much power?

"So, where is Dionysus then?" I asked. After all this time, we finally would talk to the person whom we needed to talk to.

Prometheus answered, "he is currently staying in some loft at a pub in Dublin. So who is up for a road trip?"

My hand went up quickly and Pothos chuckled. Finally, we would get some answers and I was one step closer to saving Chrys.

Chapter 9

Chrys

I did not understand how this would help.

Maka and I sat on the pink, floral, plastic-covered sofa while the three Fates fought over who would prepare the treats and tea that Maka had brought with her. Maka had offered to serve it, but they wouldn't let her, even though she was a lot better at making tea. The three of them argued over who would prepare the tea and open the box of shortbread, organize it all on the tray, and ultimately bring it into the room. This was exactly why I didn't want to come here in the first place. The incessant bickering of the Fates really brought the whole idea of a definitive idea of fate into question. They never agreed on anything, even when they were giving someone their fate. I wondered how many people they had talked to actually learned anything after they left.

Glancing around, I tried not to puke from all the pinks and flowers that decorated every inch of the room. I was not a girly-girl in the slightest and preferred black compared to this excessive floral theme. Shit, I liked anything other than this. I'd rather have something dull than the over-the-top girly theme. It felt like all the shows I had seen from the mortal world that talked about grandma's house. Is this what it was like?

Maka nudged me, probably because I had a disgusted look on my face as I was glancing around. I couldn't help it, something smelled off in here as well—probably some moldy food or a dead rat, which didn't even make sense because we were in the Underworld. I tried to turn the look into a smile when the door to the kitchen swung open. Klotho was the one carrying the tea tray out to us.

Klotho set the tray down in front of us. "Well, sweeties, what brings you out our way? Other than, of course, talking to the three of us. We are fabulous after all."

I forced myself to laugh with her and glanced at Maka to answer the question for the both of us. Honestly, I wasn't quite sure why I was there myself. I wanted to get away. I grabbed the cup and took a sip of the tea. It was dark, bitter, and I tried my best to not spit it out. Either the leaves had gone bad or this was pure burdock or something. Roots were always a hard tea to get down, other than ginger. Even then it was like drinking fire.

Maka sat up tall. "Actually, we wanted to know

whether you could see into Chrysanthemum's future. She hasn't ever had a proper fortune read to her so I figured I would bring her to the best girls in town."

The three of them looked proud. I was impressed by how easily they were flattered. Maybe this would be easier than I thought.

Also, did she have to say Chrysanthemum? These ladies would probably kidnap me because my name fit well with their decor—it being floral and all.

"Stick out your hand, young one," Lakhesis ordered.

I stuck out my hand and the three Fates all grabbed it.

They examined it, whispering words that I couldn't quite make out. It kind of hurt since they were all three trying to see me. Ugh, why did we come here again?

"Well, well," Klotho finally said, examining my hand more closely, my arm feeling as if it were going to come out of its socket. "I see the threads of love flowing through you—"

"But they are tangled and there is more than one," Lakhesis interrupted quickly. "It is hard to see where they will all eventually lead."

Klotho shot her sister a look then went on, "Yes, but there is only one true love that I can see. The other is forcefully there, not something you'd find agreeable."

"If you want me to clarify, then move over. Neither of you can see the end because that is my specialty," Atropos looked closely at my hand with an air of superiority. "Ah yes, I see it now." She licker her lips and I tried not to cringe as I saw her yellow, decaying teeth. "There's a lot of drama in your life but don't worry sweetie, it will be all right, for the one who belongs to your heart will keep you safe. And don't worry about your life, you have a long while before you have to even think about retiring."

I laughed. "But I don't even have a job yet." Because, honestly, I didn't. I may have had the power of life and death, but that was it. I wasn't a judge like my father, brought seasons to the mortal world like my mother and grandmother. I wasn't really helpful on any parts.

All three of them looked up at me, their mouth moving in unison. "Soon you will be given the task you were created for. Soon you will find your purpose. It will become your life and duty."

Eerie. I did not understand what they were trying to say, but I went with it by nodding along. It wasn't really what I wanted to know at the moment, as I could just figure that out later.

Maka spoke up. "So the man that she loves will be her lover and save her from the other string?"

Atropos nodded. "Yes, and it will be soon. Even though the other string, wire even, is strong, it is nothing compared to the true strength your soulmate has. He will untie all other knots in your life and you two will keep on traveling through life together. You have nothing to worry about."

I grinned, although I didn't know if I quite believed it. It felt like nothing was possible, that there would be no escape from my destiny to marry Zeus. But perhaps I was wrong. I only had a few months before all would be determined.

"Was that everything you wanted to learn, sweetie?" Klotho asked as she pulled my hand closer. Did these ladies not understand how much that hurt? "Because we can see much more than that."

"Yes," Lakhesis added. "There is a lot more that will be coming your way."

Atropos nodded, agreeing with her compatriot for once. "Including the shift of order—"

"That is enough."

We all turned to find a short, elderly woman standing in the doorway. All three of the Fates let go of my hand, thank the gods. I rubbed my shoulder a little.

"Sorry mother, you know how we get," Lakhesis said. If she was their mother, then that meant she was Themis, the Titaness of Divine Law and Order. She was a legend among the god world. In person, she was a lot... smaller than I imagined. I knew that didn't make a difference though, as sometimes the smallest things were the strongest.

"We just want to give her all we see." Klotho frowned.

"And so much more." Atropos folded her arms.

The woman shook her head. "The three of you, I swear, it's no wonder my hair turned grey so quickly. Now, let me see the young girl."

In an instant I was face to face with the woman. She took me off guard and I tried not to show the fear in my eyes. She stared at me, her eyes leveled even though I was sitting down.

Themis pointed straight at me. "It's you! It really is you! Thank the heavens!"

I glanced over at Maka. She shrugged. She didn't know what was going on either. At least I wasn't the only one at a loss.

Turning back to her, I asked, "What are you talking about?"

She grabbed both of my hands and pulled me towards her. "You are destined to become someone very powerful, someone who could potentially put Zeus in his place. We have needed someone who is as powerful as he is on our side. Now we have it."

I shook my head. "I am not that powerful."

"Yes you are, you are the daughter of Hades himself. He wasn't meant to have kids, you know, and then you showed up! You can control life and death! No one else can do that. No one else is allowed to do that, not even Zeus."

I was getting a little scared now. What was this woman talking about? There was no way I could put Zeus in his place. Maka didn't say a word but watched with a little amusement in her eyes.

"Yeah but I'm supposed to marry Zeus. I am engaged to him. I came here to see if there was a way out of the marriage. If there was a way I could end up with the one I love." Yes, I said it out loud. I really did care about Huntley that way and now that he was gone and I couldn't see him, I wanted to have the opportunity again.

She waved her hand aside, as if it was no big deal. "Don't worry about that, it will sort itself out in the end. But after that, you have so much potential to be a great ruler."

I shook my head. "I'm no ruler."

"Shut up, yes you are." Wow, this old lady had spunk. "Listen to me when I say to believe in yourself and everything will come with it. You will be powerful and not even Zeus will be able to stop you in the end. You will be able to do anything."

I didn't answer immediately because I really didn't feel like I would be able to. I couldn't handle Zeus earlier, and I didn't think I could handle him in the future. I just hoped that maybe she was right.

"Well," Maka put the tea cup down. "I have to get back to work and I'm sure Chrysanthemum has somewhere to be. We thank you ladies and hope you enjoyed your treats."

"Treats?" Themis turned to the table. "No one told me there were treats. You want me to starve or something?"

"You just got her mother," Lakhesis sighed. "We didn't have time to tell you about the treats."

"Thank you again, I really mean it," I said and bowed as I headed towards the door where Maka was. I wanted to get out of there as quickly as I could.

Themis replied, her mouth full of shortbread. "Don't give up, there is always a way!"

I turned and hurried out the door with Maka before they could say anything else. I gave her a dubious look.

"What's that look for? You know that it was exactly what you wanted to hear."

"Yeah, I know. But I don't know if I believe it."

She shrugged. "Well, your fate is in your hands. Just

try your hardest, all right? Now Charon is waiting for you with your stuff as I've got to go bless some people that just came to the Underworld. If you need anything, you know where to find me."

I nodded and she headed in the opposite direction. I sighed. Now I had to hear Charon's stories all over again.

Chapter 10

<u>Huntley</u>

I understood why Prometheus took so long to get back now.

He was cheap. So very cheap. I didn't understand why he couldn't just pay the extra hundred pounds to take a train straight to the ferry that would lead us to Dublin. Instead, we had to make five switches, which added another two days to our trip. I asked about where we would sleep for the five-hour layover at midnight in Edinburgh, but he just shrugged and said we would sleep at the train station.

Neither Pothos nor Mel seemed to have a problem with this, especially Mel. We could have just saved money on a seat and paid the extra hundred pounds with that since Mel always sat in Prometheus' lap. Prometheus didn't seem to care one way or another that she was there. I found it to be strange, but most relationships between the gods made little sense to me. Although, I had to admit, she was rather cute when she wasn't being crazy. I could see why a god would put up with her craziness. And after having a bedroom right next to theirs, I could kinda see why he keeps her around. Thank the gods Pothos bought me some Bose headphones.

It was kind of cool to see the countryside by train in England while heading towards Scotland. I hadn't ventured outside the city yet and felt more relaxed when the houses were spread apart. There was something to be said about nature, and how it is often ignored by people who live in the city. No one seemed to take the time to just get out here and look around and let nature do its thing. It was strange to me, given I spent most of my childhood and teen years outdoors, away from the fracas of my parents' fighting.

I wished this was just a vacation rather than us having to get somewhere to figure out how to save Chrys. I would have liked to get off at all the stops and just explore, but there was no time for that. Maybe, when all of this was over, I could travel everywhere with Chrys. Although, if I were honest, I didn't need to travel anywhere with her as just being with her was enough for me.

The worst part of our trip was when we had the layover in Edinburgh. It was from about 11pm at night until 4am. It was too late to go do anything, and contrary to what Prometheus claimed, the train station was in fact not open. We ended up buying a night's stay at some crappy bed-and-breakfast a few blocks from the station and shared one room. I didn't get any sleep, mainly because I was on the couch with Pothos and he kept kicking me in the face. I thought about wandering the streets until we had to leave, but I was a little paranoid that there might be a god or goddess out there and they would report us.

The next morning I got everyone up, since I couldn't sleep, and Mel was a bitch to wake up. She scratched and kicked and threatened eternal torture. Don't get me wrong, I hated mornings too, but damn she was scary when it came to waking up. Luckily, Prometheus was able to get her up without the entire place coming down.

"What's your problem?" Pothos asked as we boarded the train at four in the morning.

I gave him a look. "Really? I don't know, maybe it's the fact that I didn't get any sleep because someone's foot was in my face?"

"Hey, sorry, it's not like I had a choice. There was only a twin bed and the couch."

I rubbed my face as I took my seat. "Yeah, well, next time I think we should take the bed. Or, perhaps, buy another room."

Pothos laughed. "A lot of us gods like to save money if you didn't notice."

I thought about Persephone and knew that was not the case with her. "Oh yeah? Then how would you afford such an expensive flat?"

Pothos shrugged. "I don't pay for it."

That comment caught me a little off guard. I mean, I knew he couldn't have been working to pay for it all, but I figured all the gods were just somehow rich since they had powers and such.

"Then who does?"

"Aphrodite."

That made sense, especially since he was sort of related to her. I wasn't quite sure how, if he was like her son or some weird thing coming into existence that somehow connected him to her, but he usually didn't talk too much about it. He was the god of longing desire and I had a feeling that was why he hung out so much at his high school. With all those hormones going wild, there was a lot of longing to feed on, so to speak.

"Ah. That explains some things."

"And before you ask, no you don't have to worry about her showing up. She doesn't really want anything to do with me anymore. She just gives me money for food and rent in return for me not bothering her again."

I watched Pothos as he talked about Aphrodite. There seemed to be sadness in his eyes, even if he didn't voice it. I wasn't sure what was going on, but I figured if he wanted to talk about it, then he would bring it up again.

Hours upon hours and a boat-ride later, we made it to Dublin at last. It was a lot more beautiful than any of the pictures or movies I had seen. It was still raining, as it always did in the UK, but for some reason here it still seemed very colorful and not dreary like it did in

London a lot of the time. There were still tourists, as always, and I wished I could find a city where there weren't any and live there for the rest of my life.

I decided tonight I would use the credit card that Chrys had made for us for my own separate room. I didn't like using it—mainly because I wasn't sure when the credit card company would take notice and come arrest me. This money had to be coming from somewhere and having been almost caught stealing before, I really didn't want to get arrested, especially since my file would have said deceased. I had to buy a hotel room, though, or I would go insane. Hanging out with these gods with no alone time made me feel like I was going crazy.

But first thing was first, and that was to go to the small pub where Dionysus stayed. Apparently, according to the resources Prometheus had gathered, he had been staying there, alone, drinking all night and sleeping all day. Normally a pub owner would kick someone like that out, but Dionysus had a lot of cash at his disposal, unlike Prometheus who always took the cheap route.

Dublin was colder than London, which made sense since it was a bit more north than London. It was still rainy, dreary, yet colder. So much colder. I wasn't sure how the rain wasn't freezing, but it wasn't. My body sure felt like it was, though.

We made our way through the city, Prometheus leading the way. Mel was still clinging to him, not letting him out of her sight. I wasn't sure what she saw in him, especially since he wasn't returning any of her affection.

He seemed cold-hearted towards her, as if just amusing her. Maybe he didn't want to get on her bad side and just let her do what she wanted. It made sense. It also made sense that he left on his journey and just wrote us a note about what he was doing. If he told us in person, she probably would have gone with him even if he said no. She was that much of a velcro girlfriend.

We ventured down the streets of Dublin with Prometheus leading the way. He seemed to know where he was going, and I assume because he had been to Dublin before. Most of the gods had been to practically any location—I mean, that is what I would do if I were a god.

It was about 9pm and most places were starting to die down. There were very few people out, as it was the middle of the week and most had jobs to get to the next morning. Finally, we stopped at a small pub down an alleyway, away from the main drag. I wasn't even sure how they would get customers all the way down here as it was a bit dark and dank down this way and if I were to choose, I wouldn't have gone this way. The windows were unclean, filthy, and broken. Without seeming like he even noticed all these things, Prometheus stepped inside.

The inside wasn't much better. It really needed to be washed down with a hose or something, I swore. There were only two people in the pub at that moment: a disheveled red-head in the back with a few empty glasses in front of him, and a gentleman in a suit at the bar.

I started to head towards the man in the suit.

"What are you doing?" Prometheus asked. "Dionysus is over there."

"Oh…" I said. I couldn't believe a god would look so worn-out like that. I hadn't seen a god look that… human. I followed the others over.

It took Dionysus a moment, then he recognized the gods that surrounded him. He started to shake his head. "Nope. No. Not going to. Nope. Not even going to listen." He plugged his ears with his finger. "La la la la la la la—"

Prometheus struggled with him, trying to get his hands away from his ears. "Just listen to me! We can trick him, between the two of us, we can pull a fast one—"

"No! I already said I'm not doing it! Why do you think I have hidden myself away in this hellhole? I don't want the attention. I just want to stay here!"

"No you don't, you are wasting your time! Just help us right now!"

"No!"

I couldn't take any more of this stupid squabble. I grabbed Dionysus by the collar of his shirt. "Listen! There is a girl who needs our help, the daughter of Hades."

He looked at me for a second and then nodded to Mel. "You mean her? Listen, buddy, she ain't really the daughter of Hades, I don't care what she says. Her father is Zeus, who fucked Persephone disguised as Hades." He took another drink. "Because that's the type of fucked-up asshole that he is."

I shook my head. *"No*, not her. A different daughter. His only daughter."

Dionysus stared at me for a moment. Then he glanced at the others. "You all can't be serious. He doesn't have any children... He can't..."

"He does," Prometheus answered. "He hid her for millennia, but Zeus finally found out. Now he plans on marrying her and we have to help her."

Dionysus started laughing. "You are kidding me, right? You think we could stop Zeus from fucking what he wants. Why don't you talk to Hera? She's the only one who could deal with a situation like this."

Prometheus shook his head. "No, she won't. I already went down that route. Now, please, hear me out. We could finally screw that bastard over for what he has done to us."

I wondered if that was true, especially since he had never mentioned Hera before.

Dionysus stared at him for a moment, then glanced at the rest of us. "Fine, I will listen. Don't know if I will help, but I will listen to the whole story. But not here. Follow me into my office." He stood up, grabbing his beer, and lead us up the stairs.

I didn't know if we could trust this drunkard, but it was apparently worth a shot. I followed him with the others, hoping that we would finally get some answers.

Chapter 11

<u>Chrys</u>

Almost back to the palace. Almost. There.

Charon was talking my head off yet again. Although I didn't like that Father wasn't really talking to me, I kind of looked forward to the quiet sound of the Palace. I knew I would regret thinking that quickly, but I swore to the gods that if I heard one more stupid story about the weirdos Charon has lead into the Underworld, then I might just jump into the river and drown myself.

Hey, then at least I wouldn't have to marry Zeus.

The thought had crossed my mind, whether to send myself straight to Asphodel Fields. However, I knew that it wouldn't work in my favor, and that Zeus would just come and take me from there himself, not to mention I wouldn't see Huntley again, nor would I see most of the people I cared about. Father could visit, but that was about it. He didn't have the time, really, and it took a lot of power for him to return to the palace from that place. He only went there if there was some kind of crisis, which was rare. Not even I had visited the Asphodel Fields, but only saw it from afar. I had to admit, I was a bit curious as to what "paradise" was really like.

"Then there was this one time I had this couple who had died in a wreck together, they bickered the entire time, saying it was the other's fault. The girl was having an affair too, even though they had just got married. I can't tell you where they went, I think your father ended up having to judge them, I'm not sure. Nasty couple, they were. I wouldn't be surprised if they ended up in Tartarus."

I couldn't take any more of this, I swore. Why couldn't Maka have taken me with her? Or used some of her magic to teleport me back or something? I would have even been fine with helping her work rather than this. Anything is better than this. I swore she enjoyed watching me be tortured by him. She was probably using her magic to keep an eye on me and giggling to herself.

I'll get her back one of these days—in a way that doesn't make her mad at me or seek revenge. Yes, one day I would do that.

"Then there are all the men your mother snuck in here. At first, they are pretty surprised at the whole place, I guess they didn't know what the Underworld looked like. Go figure."

I really didn't want to hear this. Not after everything. I wished Charon had a mute button, if not for everything else he had told me over the years, but mainly right now because I knew there wasn't a power in the 'verse that would stop him from going on.

He went on, just as I figured. "It didn't use to be like that, though. She used to love it here, looked forward to it the entire time she was on Earth."

I gave him a look of disbelief. The idea of mother being happy here was like a myth. I couldn't never imagine it to be true. "Yeah right, ever since I've known her she's hated it here."

He shook his head. "No, for quite a while she loved it but was torn between her mother and Hades."

Maka had said the same thing and told me about how she made that tea for my mother. "Then what happened?" This was probably the first time I ever tried to press further for information from Charon. I even surprised myself. Never did I imagine I would ask Charon to keep talking.

"The stress got to be too much for her and she became the drama queen that she is now. Hades knew that it would eventually happen, especially since they filled her with lies about him and made her regret ever marrying him. I think deep down, though, she still really cares for him. It just got complicated."

I didn't care what he or Maka said, I knew in my heart I would never forgive her for the way she treated my father. It would take a lot more for me to ever care about her again. Although, at least now I could understand a little of how she was.

"Oh, here we are. Man, time sure flies when I'm with you. You should come hang out with me more often. I don't get why you don't, it's not like you have anything else to do."

"Yeah, sure whatever," I said as I grabbed my bag that now had some tea and incense in it. "I'll see if I can get away again sometime soon."

"Well just let me know and I will be there. Until then, have fun."

I gave him a half-hearted wave and headed inside the palace doors. My plan was to sneak in, get some time to myself in my bedroom, before Father realized I was back. I didn't particularly feel like helping him judge souls with the weird aura that was still between us. However, as I walked through the doors, I found him and another man waiting for me.

Wait, who was this guy? Father never hung out with anyone. By the way he presented himself, he had to be a god, but which one? It wasn't like any could travel down here, at least not that easily.

The man was rather tall, at least half of a foot taller than Father, and wore a dark blue suit with a light blue shirt underneath. I glanced down at his shoes. They were shiny—too shiny. The radiating self-important energy coming off of him was too much for me to handle. He was definitely a god.

Father was the first to talk. "Right on time, Charon said he was picking you up today, thank goodness," he added the last part under his breath. "Apparently there are some new rules you have to follow."

Oh great, Zeus was adding extra security to my own home. Fantastic. It wasn't like I could do anything, anyway.

"This is Hermes, messenger of Zeus, he will be—"

Hermes stuck his hand out to stop my father. "Um, excuse me, that is not my full title." He turned to me and had a bit of a cocky smile. "I am Hermes, Son of Zeus and Maia, God of Herds and Flocks, Travelers and Hospitality..."

Hades tried to go on. "He will be—"

"...God of Roads and Trade, Thievery and Cunning, Heralds and Diplomacy..."

Holy shit, this guy had an ego. I mean, all the gods did, but this seemed like it was a bit over the top. I looked over at Cerberus, who was gnawing on three different bones, wondering what he was up to while I was gone as Hermes went on.

"...Languages and Writing, Athletic Contests and Gymnasiums, Astronomy and Astrology..."

Father waited a moment, wondering if Hermes was finished. "*Anyway,* he will be—"

"I am the personal messenger of Zeus, who is the King of the Gods, and also I am one of the guides of the dead who leads souls down into the Underworld."

Father stared at him, looking bitter, which was surprising since he was usually good at hiding his emotions. I knew, though, that Father really hated Hermes. "Are you finished?"

Hermes turned to him and smiled. "Yes, yes I am."

He let out a sigh. "Fine, as I was saying, he will be—"

Hermes stepped in front of Father and stuck his finger out at me. "Watching over you like a hawk. Zeus knows you are up to something, he is just trying to figure out what."

Father was pinching the bridge of his nose now. I could see why he always complained when Hermes was around—he liked to make father look like a fool which was very hard to do, and Hermes made it look easy.

I examined Hermes once more. He seemed honest enough, just a bit of a troublemaker. His voice was strong, I would give him that. I bet he could persuade a lot of people to do what he wanted. He didn't have to persuade me, though, as I knew I didn't have a choice in the matter. I wondered if the Fates had seen this coming, or whether Zeus knew I went to the Fates and had sent Hermes to watch me even closer. "Okay, sounds fine to me."

Hermes paused. Apparently he wasn't used to people just going with whatever he said. That surprised me just a little, but I guess most of the other gods were more stubborn. "Well, I guess that settles it. If I believed you."

I shrugged. "Not like I have a say, and I'm already stuck here for the time being. Your job will be rather boring, just so you know."

"Oh, I believe guarding you will be one of my best jobs yet. I have to say, you must take after Persephone because you are a lot more beautiful than what I could ever imagine the daughter from this guy could ever be."

Father was fast to respond to that comment. "Touch

her and I will send you to Tartarus myself."

Hermes laughed. "Please, like I would double-cross Zeus like that. He would have my head, if not just torture me for a millennium."

Father glared at him. "I would like to think you wouldn't do anything out of respect for me."

They stared at each other in silence. Great, more drama in my life. That was all I needed. I trusted Hermes for some reason, though, and knew he cared for my father more than he was letting on. He just looked like he enjoyed pushing Father's buttons for a fun response. I have never seen Father get as worked up as he was at the moment, other than with me lately.

I couldn't stand silent any longer, so I clapped my hands together. "Well, I've had a long day of traveling, and I'm sure Hermes has too. Why don't I show Hermes his room and then take a nap in my bed? Sound good? Okay let's do that."

I must have taken them off guard as they looked at me with a blank expression for a moment then glared at each other once more. I let out a brief sigh. This would be another pain in my ass.

"Whatever, I'm heading towards the rooms. Follow me if you want Hermes."

"I'm coming," he said as he started after me.

As I began walking, I felt Father grab my shoulder to stop me. I was a bit surprised he did that and turned to him. "What is it?"

He looked at me for a moment, as if about to say something. His eyes seemed to be filled with sadness when he finally shook his head. "Nothing, never mind."

Turning quickly around, he walked in the opposite direction of us. I wondered what he was going to say but then shrugged it off. It was probably something about how I betrayed him again. I didn't want to hear that again, anyway. I just wanted some peace for once.

"Come on, Hermes, God of a bunch of shit, let me show you to your room."

Chapter 12

<u>Huntley</u>

Dionysus' room was quite nice, actually. There wasn't much to it, just a bed, desk, and wardrobe. It really surprised me that it was clean and tidy compared to what he looked. I expected an enormous mess to be quite honest.

The four of us barely fit in the room though. Prometheus took the chair, with Mel of course, and Pothos and I sat down on the floor. Dionysus sat on his bed, tired and annoyed still that we had found him.

I wondered as to the reason he was in hiding. I mean, I could imagine it had something to do with the gods being such selfish bastards and he wanted nothing to do with them anymore, but I wanted to know the details. I figured asking would get me on his bad side, and that was the last thing I needed at the moment. I would just wait and see how this went and ask Prometheus later.

Dionysus glanced at all of us, as if trying to put the pieces together already in his head. "Now, tell me what you think I would help with, but I can guarantee you it will be a big fat 'no'."

I glanced over at Prometheus, not sure if he was going to tell the tale or not. He seemed to be quiet, as if waiting for me so I told my side of the story first, even though I doubted Dionysus would listen to an account coming from, what they liked to call me, a mere human. "The daughter of Hades, Chrys, has been hiding in the Underworld all of her life. Hades has kept her close in his palace, not letting anyone who could report back to Zeus see her. From what I hear, Hermes likes to show up sometimes, so he makes things the most difficult for Hades, but Hades has always had it under control. I never have met the guy, but I have hidden Chrys from him once before.

"Hades has had many tutors for Chrys throughout the years to teach her about Earth and such. She saved me one day from floating through the rivers throughout eternity and told her father I would be the perfect tutor."

All four of them stared at me as if that was total bullshit. I definitely agreed. Pothos looked as if he was about to laugh.

I went on, a little in self-defense. "That's what she told him! I'm not saying I was a good tutor, *but* that is what happened. Anyway, she just needed some friends, I guess. When I got there, she already had one other guy around named A.J. He was some kind of king of something, a demigod. I'll get back to him in a moment."

"As you know, Persephone wasn't the greatest about sticking around the Underworld and over the centuries Chrys had begun to resent her. Chrys wanted to know why Earth was so much better and checked it out herself. I tried to talk her out of it, but A.J. pushed her to go. He had an ulterior motive to come to Earth."

I let out a deep sigh. "Come to find out, A.J. had never taken a bite of any food in the afterlife. He had waited a long time to talk Chrys into coming to Earth so he could trade her life to be immortal and never die. If I ever run into him again, I swear…"

"We will give him what he deserves, don't worry," Pothos added. "He will wish he was back in the Underworld."

I nodded. I definitely had a list of things I would do to the guy. But that could wait until after we saved Chrys.

"And what has this got to do with me?" Dionysus asked, getting impatient with the background information. He wanted to know the entire problem and yet was being impatient. People like that drove me insane.

"I'm getting to that," I replied. "Anyway, the three of us came to Earth to let her see what it was like, just for a couple of days. We were just going to get back when Pothos here tried and make a move on Chrys…"

"Hey, in my defense she was too much like Persephone, I couldn't resist."

Both Prometheus and Dionysus nodded in unison. I had to agree, Persephone was hot, but I knew how much of a bitch she could be. It didn't seem like these gods cared about personalities, though.

I went on, "So Chrys got mad and almost destroyed an entire house full of people. I was able to stop her when Mel and Prometheus showed up. Prometheus realized who, or what, she was right away and tried to get us all back to the river before Zeus learned of her but it was too late—A.J. had already alerted his father Poseidon and he tried to take Chrys for himself. He grabbed her and took her into the water, but she was able to save herself and beat the shit out of Poseidon."

"It was amazing to watch," Pothos added. "It cracks me up a little every time I think back to it. She was a badass."

Prometheus was more worried than amused. "She was killing him and bringing him back to life over and over again until Zeus stopped her with his lightning. Even then she was barely hurt."

Dionysus seemed impressed and silently was putting all the pieces together.

I continued. "So Zeus tried to kill her since he found her to be too powerful, possessing a combination of both Hades and Persephone's powers, but then Hades stepped in and attempted to stop Zeus. It was spectacular. We tried to make a run for it but Athena found us and Hades was defeated by Zeus. That's when Chrys made the deal with Zeus that she would marry him in exchange for him not hurting her or her father, giving me an immortal life, and letting her be in the Underworld when Persephone wasn't."

It was silent for a moment as Dionysus took in all the information. I wondered if he could process the entire story with how drunk he appeared. His eyes were bloodshot and I remembered anytime I was that drunk, I wasn't very coherent. Then again, he was a god. "I don't see what this has to do with me."

Prometheus was the one to explain. "Because we don't want her to be in Zeus' hands, he doesn't deserve her, not to mention he shouldn't be the one to decide if a god is too strong or not. He is just afraid of the prophecy and the chance that his title could get taken away from him."

"You mean the prophecy of a child born of death and light becoming the most powerful god of them all, even more powerful than Zeus himself?" Dionysus asked.

We all nodded in unison. That pretty much summed it up.

Dionysus glanced at each of us. "But if she is that powerful, why doesn't she just take Zeus out?"

I responded, "she doesn't know how to control her powers fully yet, as Hades was too scared for her to do something that would alert Zeus."

"You mean like kill and bring back Poseidon, the ability to command life and death, making her one of the strongest gods in existence?"

I nodded. "Yeah, like that."

Dionysus rubbed his eyes. "Look, I can't help you. There is no way to get her out of this marriage, not when Zeus is involved. Your best bet would be to simply let her decide her fate. If she really wanted out of it, she would just destroy him."

I couldn't believe what I was hearing. Why did everyone shy away from helping when it came to Zeus? Why did none of them stand up to him? If they believe she could make a change, if they really believe she was as great as she was, why wouldn't they have a little faith and have her back?

I stood up. "No! I have not come all this way for you to tell me there is nothing we can do. There has to be a way!"

"Look, kid, you are just a human. You don't get it, you don't know what it is like to be cursed by Zeus, to have to deal with centuries of torment. There's a reason he is called the King of Gods, because he's our ruler. There has to be a damn good reason to cross him for us, and your girlfriend isn't a good reason for me."

I wanted to punch him, but Pothos grabbed me. "Come on, Huntley, let's see if we can find someone else to help us."

I let out a sigh and glared at Dionysus for a moment, then turned towards the door with the others.

"But, I mean, if I were in your position..." Dionysus began. I faced him, wondering if he would help us. After that speech, I didn't think he would offer anything. "That's to say, I have no part in this. But if you were me... Divorce isn't allowed. Multiple lovers and partners, yes, but divorce isn't a thing for us gods. We are stuck if we are married, which is why Zeus is hoping for two wives. But if you were to, let's say, marry Chrys before her marriage with Zeus, then perhaps it would stop this wedding. I don't know how easy that will be since I have a feeling she is being watched constantly. Maybe you could even say the marriage happened before this all happened. Might not work, but it may be worth a shot."

I couldn't believe what I was hearing. "So if I married her—"

He let out a sharp laugh. "Ha! No, not you. You are a human, he would just flick you off like a bug, say the marriage didn't count, and marry her anyway. No, it would have to be some really powerful, someone who has been around longer than Zeus has..." Dionysus stared straight at Prometheus.

Prometheus quickly shook his head. "No, you don't mean me."

"Has to be. I mean, if you wanted it to work. But it wasn't me who gave you this idea, right? Besides, you will also need to figure out a way to get married for it to actually work. Zeus will see through your lies. Persephone would be your best bet to help, since she was able to marry Hades before anyone had a say. Granted most say Hades tricked her into doing it, but that is a complete and utter lie. Besides, Persephone is the only one who can get you into the Underworld."

"Oh great..." I whispered. I didn't want to see her again, and she probably didn't want to see me after I had yelled at her in public. And in front of her mom.

Dionysus nodded to the door. "Now get going before someone sees you. I don't need any unnecessary drama."

Prometheus bowed his head a little. "Thank you, old friend."

With that, we left Dionysus alone and ventured back to London.

Chapter 13

<u>Chrys</u>

Hermes wasn't *th*at bad. He was just... full of himself. But at least he was fun to a point. Especially if Father was around.

I didn't know the entire story between Hermes and my Father, but it was definitely entertaining. I concluded that the chief reason Father hated him was because Hermes could get into the Underworld without Hades figuring out how he did it. This made Hermes quite proud of himself, which then led him to make fun of Father even more.

And Father definitely deserved it these past few days.

Father still wasn't speaking to me since Hermes got here, but tended to talk more to Hermes if we were all in the same room, which wasn't often to be honest. It mainly was just around dinner time if we all was eating in the dining hall at the same time. We would both try to pick a time, the other wouldn't be there, but then we ended up picking the same times out of sheer coincidence. It kind of made me realize Father and I thought the same way. I wasn't sure if it made me happy or a little frustrating.

I sort have wished I stayed at Maka's place a bit longer, but she had several jobs in helping the blessed come to the Underworld and I didn't want to bother her, not to mention if Hermes had to wait for me to get back then he might think I was doing something suspicious. I guess we were since we saw the Fates, who told me that everything would turn out for the best and that I would end up marrying the one I truly loved. Which was Huntley.

I tried my hardest not to think about him, as it just made me more miserable. At least I had Hermes now to take my mind off of it. Although I didn't like being watched constantly, especially since I wanted to find a way out of the marriage, at least now I had some company. And Hermes was hilarious.

Hermes and I were sitting at the dining room table. He commented on how Hades must have been compensating for something since this room was so grand and he doubted anyone ever came to visit. Father, thank goodness, wasn't around this time. It felt weird, though, sitting here without him when just months ago we ate happily together. Our relationship was perfect, if a father-daughter relationship ever could be perfect. We talked, mainly about tutoring and the job, never about Huntley, and for the most part I could be honest with him. I mean, when Huntley was involved I wasn't quite that honest, especially with my feelings, and where I had found him… and about the pomegranate seeds. Okay, so maybe our relationship wasn't perfect, but it was way better than most people's relationships—especially with these gods.

For dinner that night, the chef had made us some cottage pie, an English specialty, although it had a lot more flavor in this one. I hadn't had it since we were in London, which made me miss Huntley even more. Damn this irony.

"So, Chrys, what was it like being stuck down here for so long? Must have been torture as this place is quite drab," Hermes asked as he took a bite of his food. "But wow, the food is fantastic. I guess when you rule the dead, you can get them to do whatever you want, huh?"

I shrugged. "I don't know, the chefs seem to like working in the palace here. They change people every few months, when they are sick of cooking for us, and Father sends them off to paradise, then brings new ones in. They have all been quite wonderful to us over the years."

"Well, that's surprising. From what Demeter says, Persephone has told her some horrific stories about this place."

So he was one of those gods who believed everything they heard, and always sided with Olympus, but I guess

I already figured that since he was helping Zeus out. "Mother may not like it here, but I do. Or Demeter was lying to everyone since she forced Persephone to choose between Hades and her own mother, although I know who I would choose."

Hermes eyes widened, as if caught off guard by my comment, then laughed. "I should have figured you were a 'Daddy's girl' with all the black clothes and angsty attitude. You are just like him."

I retorted sharply. "The only reason he seems angsty is because he doesn't like dealing with all you drama-queen gods. I can understand why he hid me away from them for so long."

"Oh poor Hades didn't want his daughter to learn about the real world and how dark and depressed he really is compared to us."

I stood up and slammed my hands on the table. I could feel the dark energy in my hands and tried not to let it escape. I doubted Hermes would let it slide if I let some of that energy out on him. "My father is not dark and depressed!"

As I yelled at Hermes, I saw Father walk into the dining room. I was quiet for a moment as we looked at each other when he finally sighed.

"Hermes, are you trying to talk my daughter into hating me?"

Hermes shrugged. "What can I say, it's my gift."

I sat down as my father went on. Here came another argument between the two. "More like it's all of you other gods' purpose in life to make me look bad. It's what you all did to Persephone."

"Look, you knew as well as the rest of us she didn't belong here. She is the goddess of fertility, an Earthly goddess, and you are the God of the Underworld. In what dimension did you ever think that would work?"

"Love knows no bounds."

I was surprised my father would say something like that. I honestly didn't think he cared that much about Persephone anymore, as they always fought since I could remember. What was she like in his eyes? Did he still see her as the woman he first married? Why was she never that woman when I was around? It made me blame myself a little, as I felt I had caused a lot of stress in both of their lives. However, now meeting the other gods, it was probably more the stress they put on her rather than me.

Hermes took another bite. "Yeah, well, look where that love left you. Still all alone, miserable, with a daughter who was so reckless that she ended up getting engaged to Zeus."

Father didn't say another word as he grabbed his plate of food and left the dining hall. I thought about saying something, but I knew it wouldn't help. Hermes had really struck a chord with him this time.

But I did wonder why everyone seemed to hate my father so much and why he put up with their shit. I guess originally it was all for me and that was why he had hidden me for so long. He had to have known that I couldn't stay hidden forever, though. Someone would have eventually found out even if I hadn't screwed up. I mean, Hermes had almost found me out a few times already.

Father probably took his food to eat in his study alone. I felt bad for him right now, to be so alone that all the other gods made fun of him. I wished I could do something—I wished I could get out of this marriage and be able to keep him company. I wanted to tell him about what the Fates had said and how they knew I could end up with the one I loved. Okay, that last part I didn't want to tell him as he would never approve of me marrying a human. I had a feeling though he would approve of that instead of Zeus. Eventually we would have to go down that road and I wasn't looking forward to that.

Whatever. First, I had to stop this marriage .

"Hermes," I began. "Why exactly is it that everyone in Olympus hates my father?"

He shrugged, as if it wasn't a big deal—as if everyone knew to hate him. "I guess you wouldn't see it, especially since you grew up here, but your father is a bit of recluse. He has shut himself away, hiding from the rest of the gods. That was even before the battle against Kronos. On top of that, he brings darkness and death wherever he goes. When he steps on the Earth, you probably didn't notice, but things start to die. Plants die, trees die, I hate to see what would happen if he pet Bambi."

Funny, I didn't notice, but I was a little preoccupied. With that knowledge, though, I kind of wondered how my mother could have loved him in the first place. Hermes had pointed out that she was the Goddess of

Fertility—why would she love someone who brought death to the things she created?

"So because of his powers you see him as someone to ridicule? That makes sense. Hate to wonder what everyone thinks of me, especially after what I did to Poseidon."

I had to admit, the power I used against Poseidon even surprised me. I never knew I could bring death and life like that. And I *couldn't* say it out loud, but it felt good. I just wished I had a bit more control over it.

Shaking his head, he went on. "It wasn't just his powers. He never let anyone get close, so no one knows what he is thinking. On top of that, he kidnapped Persephone and hid her down here until we came down to save her."

I stared at him. Kidnapped? What was he talking about?

"That's not the story I heard," I said.

Hermes chuckled a little. "Yeah, well, who told you that story? Hades? I'm sure he thinks he's not the villain in that tale."

"Actually, I've heard the story from both of them. Separately. Although Mother acts like she regretted it, she never said he ever kidnapped her. She ran away with him."

"Whatever you say."

"She wouldn't lie to me, not when she acts like she hates it here all the time."

"You think she would tell her daughter the truth—that she was kidnapped, forced into marriage with the God of the Underworld, all the while Demeter cried for her child and stopped at nothing to find her, to only have her nine months of the year? You think your mother would admit that to you as a child?"

Mother never hid anything from me—not her feelings, not how much she hated the Underworld after being here for so many years, and how she was sick of Hades. If she really hated it from the beginning, she would have told me to get me on her side.

"Yes, she would have."

Hermes stared at me for a moment, then laughed. "You are one interesting kid, you know that? I think we are going to have a lot of fun in the next few months."

I had forgotten for a moment what this was all about—why he was here. He was here to keep an eye on me, to make sure I wouldn't try to escape my prospective marriage with Zeus.

And yet they acted like my father was the bad guy here.

Chapter 14

<u>Huntley</u>

So we were back right where we started.

The part that sucked about being back in London and realizing that we needed Persephone to help us was the fact that I had just saw her a few days before we found out we needed her. And that I had yelled at her and blamed her for everything. In front of her mother no less. Why did he always make things more difficult? It was my curse, I guess.

Pothos and I were at the flat, grabbing some food to snack on before heading out to the streets to find Persephone. I hadn't told them yet about what had happened, and how I had yelled at her about how worthless she was. And how she was a shitty mom. I didn't particularly want to tell Prometheus since he would just call me a stupid human. Pothos would at least understand where I was coming from.

Prometheus and Mel had already gone out to search for Persephone, or at least that is what they said they were doing. I didn't doubt they would eventually get around to it, or just keep an eye out for her, but were actually just spending the day out and about. At least they were out of my hair now.

Pothos and I would check South Kensington, where I saw her last. He figured she would be in that area because of Harrods. I bit my tongue on how I already knew that until we were alone.

As Pothos lathered jelly on his PB&J, I finally told him the truth. "Hey Pothos, I already ran into Persephone like a week ago."

His eyes darted over at me. "What?"

"I ran into her near Harrods like a week ago."

He put down the spreading knife. "What did you do?"

"Okay, why do you assume I did something?"

"Well, did you?"

I nodded. "Yeah."

"That's why. Damn it Huntley, why can't you ever keep your mouth shut?"

I shrugged. "I don't know, honestly. I mean you would think of how many times my parents hit me for back-talking, something would have stuck."

Pothos sighed. "I swear, what am I going to do with you? Seriously, you realize you could have pissed her off so much that she will never talk to us again, right?"

I knew that and it had been eating away at me. I wanted to tell him earlier but I knew he would be pissed, just like he was now. But now at least Prometheus wouldn't be here to judge me.

"You make fun of Mel all the time," I commented, even though I knew it had nothing to do with this conversation. I was just trying to make myself feel better.

"That is different and you know that. We are friends, sort of, and she gets free rent. She chooses to put up with my bullshit."

He had a point. I was actually the one to be staying at Persephone's home for free for a few years. Now that I thought about it, was I staying there for free since I was dead? I guess it really was Hades' home.

"What was it like living with her?" Pothos asked. "I know it isn't relevant to the situation but I have always been curious."

I shrugged. "I don't know, I didn't see her that often. She was there only for three months and usually was off doing her own thing or sleeping with men she had sneaked into the palace."

"So it's true that she does that? I never would imagine that Hades would let her get away with it."

"He doesn't seem to care. He puts up with a lot of shit. I think he keeps his cool for Chrys to be honest, or because he's in a shitty situation. They still... Never mind. Anyway, I think their relationship is more complicated than they let people know."

"Huh. Go figure," Pothos sighed. "She puts up a good front I guess. I can see into her mind though. I wonder what holds her back from expressing her true feelings."

"What do you mean?" I asked.

He shook his head. "Never mind, forget I said anything. I'm not supposed to be diving into the minds of any gods, or at least that's what was ordered of me."

"And you didn't consider Chrys to be a god?"

"I technically didn't know at the time. Or at least, I didn't know what god she was. Can you go a day without bringing that up?"

"Nope."

"Whatever, finish making your sandwich so we can head out okay?" We have a lot of work to do since you probably blew our chance with Persephone."

I didn't say another word but finished making my grilled cheese sandwich. I wasn't one for PB&Js.

Once we finished our sandwiches, Pothos and I took the Underground towards Harrods. Pothos glared at me anytime I appeared to be opening my mouth to talk to one of the workers who yelled at me for using my card wrong or something. I kept my mouth shut around him since I knew he would hit me otherwise.

We made it to Harrods and searched around the mall. I had been on the outside many times and never saw what the big deal was, but when we went inside, I finally understood.

Holy. Shit.

There were parts of it that were like a fucking Egyptian mansion movie set. I couldn't believe what I was seeing. It didn't look like anyone was actually buying anything, as when I saw one of the price tags, I about died. $1000 for a stupid dress? Are you kidding me? This was ridiculous. Most people were only here to see the glamor.

But at least there was an ice cream shop.

The cool thing about being immortal was that I didn't feel like I was eating bad when I had ice cream and cheese all day. It was great. The same happened in Hades' Palace, since my body was already dead and yet at the same time I would find myself hungry at times. I still didn't get how that worked.

I still couldn't believe A.J. had ate nothing in the couple of thousands of years he had been down there. It seemed unbelievable.

There was no sign of Persephone, although that wasn't much of a surprise. Even if she was here, this place was like a maze. The odds of running into her were quite slim.

"What if we made an announcement over the microphone? Have the information desk say her son was lost or something?" I asked Pothos as we made our way through the watch section. Who knew there were so many different expensive watches in the world.

"Why would she ever fall for that? She doesn't have a son and would figure it was a set up."

He had a point. Persephone was smarter than that, I agreed. I was mostly just going through all the options I had at the moment.

We finally made it through the entire mall and didn't run into Persephone, or any other god for that matter. I was kind of surprised, since this seemed to be the spot for all the rich gods to gather.

"She's not here," Pothos sighed. "Let's head over to SOHO."

"How far is that?" I asked. I really didn't want to take the Underground again.

Pothos shrugged. "I don't know, about 3 or so kilometers."

I stared at him blankly. "In miles?"

"I don't know, I gave you a phone didn't I? Look it up."

I pulled out the iPhone Pothos had let me have of his so he could upgrade to the newest model. I googled the conversion and found that it was only two miles. "Can we walk?"

"Yes."

Pothos didn't want to deal with another scene in the Underground. I let out a little laugh as we headed outside and towards SOHO.

It rained the entire walk over, as usual. This rain never stopped, I swore. Pothos had an umbrella and didn't get that wet, but I just had my jacket on. About halfway there, Pothos made me get under the jacket since he didn't want to deal with me getting his home all dirty when we got back. Crazy thing in London, everyone used an umbrella. In the United States, people frowned upon it until they were tourists. It was really strange, but it was in their genes.

When we got to the SOHO district, the weather calmed down and we were able to come out from underneath the umbrella. We got a couple of looks from people, thinking that Pothos and I were a couple. I didn't care that we shared the umbrella and they could just shove it up their own asses as far as I cared. It wasn't any of their business.

SOHO was more fascinating than Harrods, at least for my taste. SOHO was mainly an entertainment district and had a lot more range of people. I liked the colors of the different shops and how they tried to stand out from the rest, although it made them all look alike because they each stood out.

I wasn't quite sure how we would check a theatre district, as we weren't going to go interrupt a play and whatnot to look for Persephone. I guess in reality we were just grasping at straws to find where Persephone was.

"I don't think she's here," I commented as we turned down another street. "I mean, do you think she would stick around London still?"

"You mean because you chewed her out a week ago? I really doubt a human like you would matter to her, but that doesn't mean she wasn't already leaving the area to go somewhere."

Pothos had a point. She could have just been in the area for a couple of days, and then left, not to mention London was a big city. "Where do you think she could have gone?"

"I don't know, of anyone, you know her best, or at least have seen her the most compared to us. You should be the one that knows."

"I never really talked to her, she was always picking

fights with Hades and Chrys and kept away from them. I mostly spent that time keeping Chrys company which she was crying in her room after she had a fight with Persephone."

"Hades let you be with her daughter alone in her room? Damn, that man must really trust you. I wouldn't, but that's mostly because I can see into your mind."

I shot him a look. "Hey, I thought you said you weren't supposed to be doing that."

"No, I said that I wasn't supposed to be doing that to gods. Besides, I don't have to look inside your head to know that was what you were thinking."

I couldn't argue with him there.

"It's a wonder why neither of you put a move on each other yet, it's not like she didn't want it either."

I was starting to get irritated. "How about we drop the subject for the time being?"

"Whatever, was just making small talk."

"Yeah, well, you're irritating me."

"When is someone not irritating you? You need to let loose."

I ignored his last comment and took a seat near a park, watching as people walked past. Pothos took a seat next to me. We sat there, silent, keeping an eye out for anyone who could look like Persephone.

"We will find her, don't worry," Pothos whispered.

I really hoped he was right. I didn't want to imagine what would happen if we didn't find her. We needed to get to the Underworld and tell Hades of our plan, or something like that. I didn't like the idea of Prometheus possibly marrying Chrys, or making it look like she was marrying him, but it was the only shot we had, and it was much better than her marrying Zeus.

Just as I was about to give up for the day I saw a person at the corner of my eye. It looked like Persephone. She had just mixed in with the crowd and I hurried after her as Pothos called after me.

This was my only chance.

Chapter 15

Chrys

I regretted saying I wished I had someone to hang out with in the palace. Hermes was great and all, but I really needed some alone time now. I just needed a happy medium for once in my life, but that was never going to happen.

He was around me constantly, the only time that I was truly alone was when I was asleep, but I knew he was just on the other side of the wall, making sure I didn't sneak out. I was glad at least I didn't have to share a room with him or anything, but still I was going a little crazy. At night I had alone time, but I still felt like I was being watched. It felt like he was consistently outside of my door, listening. I hated it.

The other problem was that not only was he a stranger to me, but he was also someone who was there to report back to Zeus. He didn't feel like someone who I could grow familiar with due to fear that he would tell whatever I said to Zeus. So instead I felt even more alone when I was with him, which sucked.

Currently we were sitting in the rec-room, playing a board game. I picked out the *game Ticket to Ride: E*urope as Hermes had never played it before and I was getting rather bored with just killing time around the palace. I judged a few days with Father, but he was giving me more problems than usual, making comments under his breath about Hermes being there so I didn't want to bother him anymore. All I needed was for him to be even more mad at me.

I burned some incense that Maka had given me since it helped me relax. Father should be judging the dead right now so he wouldn't notice the incense. Even if he did, I wouldn't really care.

"So, how do you play this game?" Hermes asked as I set up the board. He grabbed a handful of popcorn as he watched me sort the trains and separate the cards.

"It's easy, you try to get tickets with the same colored trains to complete a track. You also take route cards and try to complete those routes on the board." I handed him the rules. "Here, these probably explain it better than I can."

He glanced over the rules quickly then laughed. "Alright then, makes sense. But you do realize that I am the God of Travelers, Roads, and Trade, right? This is practically a game meant for me."

I shook my head sarcastically. "No, I had no idea what you were the god of. Haven't heard it a billion times in this past week or anything."

"Very funny. But my point still stands—you are not going to win."

Shrugging, I went on. "We will see. I could win as I have played this more times than you have. And I'm pretty good at it. You probably won't win."

Hermes appeared a little offended, which I found a little amusing. "I'd like to see you try. Let's begin."

He let me start first. He acted like it was because he was a gentleman, but I knew it was because he was a little confused about the game and wanted me to show him how it was played. I hoped that I would win just to make him mad, but that would mean I would have to outsmart him, or get lucky with the cards. Either way, only time would tell.

Once we had done a few rounds back and forth, he began to get a better understanding of the game. I think he realized it wasn't only strategy, but it had to do with the luck of what train cards you drew as well, which made winning a little more difficult. He was trying really hard to give the appearance the game was no big deal, and it made me smile a little more. Playing a game was a good idea and it really lifted my spirits. But in the back of my head, I kept realizing why he was truly here.

He was spying for Zeus.

The game went on for a while and I had the lead. It was hard in the end to tell who was really winning as there were cards with points hidden from each other. I wondered how many points he had from finished routes as I had just finished all of mine.

"I'm going to grab new routes to add to my previous ones," I announced when it was my turn. His eyes widened.

"You can do that?"

I nodded. "Yup."

He looked at his cards again, then bit his lip. I doubt he had his finished, but was trying to figure out if he could grab more routes or not.

I looked down at the cards I grabbed. I already had one route done from the ones I grabbed, so I set that down in my pile. I studied the other two, debating if I should pick either of them. One had just an extra city to get to and the other was a totally different route. It was possible to do and it was only a few points that if I lost it wouldn't affect me much. If I took all three cards, I figured Hermes would freak.

So I took all three cards.

He just stared at me, looking worried, then put his cards down. "Fine, I will grab a new route too."

I gestured towards the cards and he grabbed his three. As he looked at the cards, he smacked his head on the table.

I laughed. "Hey, I think we should totally play Poker later. You have a great game face."

"Shut up."

We were both laughing at this point when I noticed something out of the corner of my eye. I glanced over to find my father standing there watching us. I hadn't heard him come in and wondered as to why he wasn't in the Throne Room judging souls.

He nodded to the board. "Seems you two are having fun."

I glanced at the table where the game was and shrugged. "Figured we would kill some time and play a game."

"Kill time? Now you just sound like your mother."

I bit my lip. I could tell Hermes wanted to make a comment but didn't. Ugh, not this again. I didn't want to start a fight with him, so I tried to ignore his comment. "Want to join us?"

"And play with Hermes? No thank you."

I kept telling myself to calm down and let it go. "Then why are you here?"

He stayed in the doorway, not stepping any closer. "I was wondering where you were. I figured maybe you would show up to help me judge."

Nope. I couldn't stay calm with him anymore. I had to respond to his nonsense, "And I thought you made it clear that I wasn't wanted there. You seem to hate being around me after I disobeyed you, so I have kept my distance."

Hermes stayed quiet, knowing better than to get in the middle of a father and daughter fight. I couldn't blame him, I didn't want to be in the middle of this fight either.

"Well it's more him I don't want to see. I never said I didn't want you around. I'm just frustrated at what you did."

"Yeah and I hate feeling that energy coming off of you constantly! I don't deserve that!"

I was standing up now, face flushed. I thought carefully, making sure more power didn't reach my mind. If I started to see red, then I probably would lose all control. At least I knew I couldn't hurt my father as he was the God of the Underworld.

Hermes put his cards on the table and just played with his nails, listening in.

Father stepped forwards towards me. "Well I don't deserve to have people in my life leaving me alone all the time!"

I hadn't heard him yell in a long time, especially not at me. He kept his voice down usually and the only time I did hear him yell was at mother.

"I'm not leaving you alone, I made it so I was here most of the year!" I exclaimed back at him. I didn't understand why he couldn't get it through that thick skull of his.

"But you still have to leave me for that piece of shit brother of mine!"

What the fuck was he talking about? I could feel bits of my power leaking through my fingers. I noticed Hermes stare and lean back a little farther in his chair.

I yelled back at my father. "Not by my choice!"

The air buzzed with anger and dark energy. I wasn't the only one that was losing control. We both tried to take deep breaths, but it wasn't helping.

Father pointed at the incense. "What is that? What did I tell you about that incense?"

Now he was just grasping at straws. He wasn't able to keep his cool any longer.

"To not burn it while you are around. Sorry, I didn't think you would come looking for me since you have been ignoring me most of the time for the past few months."

He pinched the bridge of his nose. "I can't deal with this anymore, you are giving me a headache just like Persephone."

"Well, maybe I am just like her! Maybe I will turn into her and bitch about living here for the rest of my existence!"

"Probably since everyone around here doesn't listen!" he yelled back.

I slammed my fist on the table. Train pieces went everywhere. Hermes quickly grabbed them and tried to put them back where he thought they went.

"Damn it, Father, why can't you just forgive me for the one shit-ass decision I made? Or maybe this cold shoulder of yours is the exact reason no one likes you!"

He didn't say anything for a moment, then shook his head. "Fine, Chrys, if you feel that way I'll leave you alone."

Father turned and left as tears started to flow down my face. I let them come without reacting to anything, just like usual. Being a god was learning how to ignore sadness and pain. I turned back to the game Hermes and I were playing.

"Who's turn is it?" I asked, my face still wet from the tears.

Hermes looked at me for a moment. "Do you want to talk?"

I shook my head. "No. Let's just finish this game. I don't want to think about him anymore."

"It's your turn."

"Okay, let's see then…" I looked at my hand and tried to figure out what to do next without curling up in a ball and crying. "I will pull some train cards, I guess."

Chapter 16

Huntley

I was still trying to catch up to the woman I saw that looked like Persephone. She had the same long brown hair, a tan coat, and heels. Her facial structure looked almost perfect, which was what first caught my eye.

She was strutting fast, as if in a hurry. I wondered if she had seen me and didn't want to get yelled at again. I felt like an idiot for treating her the way I did now that she was the key to freeing Chrys. I guess I didn't know it at the time, but I still felt like a fool.

As Persephone, or at least the person whom I thought was Persephone, rounded the corner, I hurried after her. As I went around the corner myself, she was nowhere to be seen. Shit. I glanced all around but didn't see any trace of her hair or coat anywhere.

"Huntley, seriously, what is wrong with you?" Pothos finally caught up with me.

I turned to him and sighed. "I thought I saw her."

Pothos put his hand on my shoulder. "We will find her eventually, don't worry."

I tried to believe that was true, but deep down I couldn't see it happening. She was probably long gone— I mean, I know I would be if I were her. Even though I knew she deserved it, I felt a little bad that I called her out on all her shit. It wasn't my place, but when did I ever listen to things like that? I always spoke out when I shouldn't say anything.

Pothos and I searched through SOHO one more time, and I didn't try to avoid people as they walked towards me—bumping straight into them. I got quite a few cuss-words thrown my way by strangers, and then Pothos. Pothos ended up grabbing me every time I was about to run into someone. He didn't want to deal with it anymore.

We toured around the surrounding neighborhoods, although most of them were residential. I wondered if there were any other gods that we could find that would know where Persephone was, and wouldn't tell Zeus we were asking. Prometheus did have that memory wipe potion, so we could use that on whoever we asked. I figured the best idea would be to ask him when we got back. However, I could ask Pothos now if he knew anyone.

"Pothos, is there anyone we could ask that would tell

us where Persephone is? Like a friend or something?"

He cringed. "No."

"That was a lie."

"No as in there is no one we could ask. There are a few that would know their whereabouts, but none that would willingly tell us, not to mention they would be more trouble than anything. So no, there isn't."

His comment made me even more curious. I wanted to learn more about these people but decided not to push it. If he didn't even want to deal with them, and he dealt with Mel on a daily basis, they had to be bad. Although, if they hung out with Persephone, I figured, they had to be of bad character.

It was starting to get late, the streetlights flickering on and the sun, wherever it was behind the clouds, was darkening the sky. We stopped in front of a park that was near the entrance to the Underground and glanced at all of the people that were leaving work and now heading home, or to the pub, for the day.

That's when I swore I spotted her. She was wearing the same jacket from the other day and had the same curled hair.

I bolted after her, Pothos cussing yet again.

Bumping into a few people, I rushed towards her, hoping that maybe we had been lucky this time and maybe we had finally found her. Then she could help us get into the Underworld and I could see Chrys again.

I was inches away now from her. I didn't know if I should yell her name or put my hand on her shoulder or if I should just try to hop in front of her. She was still walking pretty fast. Once I was able to reach out and touch her, I put my hand on her shoulder.

"Persephone, wait!"

She turned and I gulped. It wasn't Persephone, it was just some person in the same type of coat. She was definitely the person I had seen earlier, so Persephone was nowhere to be seen. I was wrong.

"Sorry, I thought you were someone I knew," I said.

She stared at me for a moment, then said. "You said Persephone, what an odd name for a person. Girlfriend I presume?"

I shook my head. "No, but her mother. I said something I shouldn't have said to her and wanted to apologize." I still wasn't a hundred percent convinced that this person wasn't Persephone, so I wanted to show her that I wasn't there to cause trouble.

"Well, I hope you find her. I bet she would appreciate you apologizing."

With that, she turned away and headed off in another direction. I sighed as Pothos caught up to me once again. He was out of breath this time.

"Damn it Huntley, what did I say? We need to do this together! You can't just run off from me."

"It doesn't matter, it wasn't her." I kicked a pebble off of the street and towards the grass. "It was stupid of me to think it was."

Pothos glanced over at the woman and didn't say anything. He seemed like he was concentrating on something. I looked to where he was staring and realized he wasn't staring at the woman, but at a group of men that were heading towards us.

"Shit," I breathed out. "I told you this always happened when it started to get dark out.

"And I said I believed you."

"Whatever. What should we do now? They are blocking the direction towards the Underground." I didn't doubt that the two of us could take them, but I don't particularly want to get arrested for being in a fight.

"The great thing about London, Huntley, is there are a lot of places to run, and a lot of ways to access the Underground." He grabbed my arm and pulled me in the opposite direction of the five punks that were headed our way. "Now come on, let's get out of here."

We ran down the streets, Pothos now, not caring if we ran into any strangers. The five men were now running at us, shouting at the surrounding people to stop us. None of them answered their request.

Except for the tall man in the suit.

He grabbed both of us by the collars of our shirts and pulled us into a dark alleyway. Why no one tried to stop him, or even noticed, I wasn't sure. It was that city attitude, I supposed.

Pothos screamed, which sort of surprised me. I didn't think a god would get scared enough to scream. That is, until I looked over at who grabbed us.

Shit. It was the guy I had seen in Hyde Park earlier, the God of War. Ares.

Now that I had a better look, because his face was now in both of ours, I could see the anger in his eyes. I recognized the anger, mainly because I had seen it many times in the mirror. I wondered what his story was—how he became the God of War, and where this anger stemmed from.

But that would be for another time, because right now I doubted he would answer any of my questions.

Neither Pothos nor I fought his grip, mainly because we knew we couldn't do anything about it. He was the God of War. Even I wasn't stupid enough to try to piss him off, or at least piss him off even more.

"What do we have here?" Ares asked as he dragged us down the alleyway a little further, behind some dumpsters so no one passing by on the street could see. This was the end, I swore. He was going to turn us in to Zeus and we would never be able to save Chrys. Fuck.

Pothos spoke, his voice shaking a bit. "Hey buddy, long time no see."

"I swear to Zeus if you try anything Pothos, you are a dead man," Ares growled.

"I would never do that... again. You know she kicked me out for screwing with people's heads—mainly you two. I would never do it again, I learned my lesson. I swear it!"

Great, Pothos was already on his bad side. The more I learned about him, the more I realized he was as much of a trouble maker as me.

"Why are those possessed men after you?" he asked. So they were possessed. That answered that question.

Pothos smiled half-heartedly. "Good question. Has to do with the daughter of Hades, probably, and Zeus. And us."

Ares looked like he wanted to squash Pothos into a pulp. He kept his fists clenched around the collars of our shirts as he shoved us against the brick wall.

"What are you talking about?"

This guy hadn't heard? I guess he wasn't planted in London to spy on us. At least we had that going for us. Also, I figured news traveled a little quicker in the godly realm. I guess I was wrong—or maybe some just didn't keep up with the gossip. I could see the God of War being a bit of an outcast like Hades. No one wanted to talk to him because no one wanted to get on his bad side.

"Ummm, Huntley, how about you explain?" Pothos' voice cracked a little. I did sort of enjoy seeing him scared like this, even though we both were probably about to die.

I went through everything as quickly as I could. "Hades had a daughter that no one knew about. Zeus found out and was going to destroy her. Instead, he decided he was going to take her for his wife. Zeus probably has been keeping an eye out on us since we are trying to stop the wedding so he sends spies to try to knock some sense into us."

Yeah, that pretty much summed it up. I was glad I was able to explain in just a few sentences since this guy didn't appear to want to hear the details, or listen to me drag on about it.

Ares eyes narrowed. "Zeus is taking another wife?"

Pothos and I nodded in unison.

Ares' face started to turn red. Oh god, we were dead.

"But the gods can only have one partner, that is what he always says."

Pothos answered. "Right, that's what I said. Apparently he thinks he can bend all the rules."

Ares let go of our shirts, and both Pothos and I collapsed to the ground. Maybe he wasn't going to kill us after all. I had no idea what was going to happen next, I was so confused.

"After all this time!" Ares yelled out, more at nothing than at us. "He decided to bend his fucking rules. Well, I'm not standing for that!" He turned to us. "What are you doing to stop it?"

The question caught me off guard. I didn't know how to respond. Pothos answered. "We are looking for Persephone. We need to talk to her."

"Right. And as for these punks…" Ares turned and decked one of the men that had been chasing us right in the jaw with his fist. How he knew they were just rounding the corner, I had no idea. I guess he was the God of War after all. "I'll take care of them. You just get back to your flat."

He didn't have to tell us twice. Pothos and I fled the scene as Ares beat the shit out of the five guys.

Chapter 17

<u>Chrys</u>

I lay in bed, staring up at the starry-painted ceiling, wondering what I was going to do.

I couldn't sleep and I particularly didn't want to roam around since I might get spotted by Hermes and accused of plotting against Zeus. I mean, I was, in a way, but that wouldn't have been the case this time. Especially since I knew I couldn't do anything for the time being, especially in the Underworld. What I really needed to do was get better at controlling my powers so that maybe I could in fact defeat Zeus and take down his dictatorship.

Yeah, that probably wasn't going to happen.

It wasn't necessarily that I thought that I wasn't strong enough, which was partly true, but it was more the fact that if I did fail, then I would be sent to Tartarus. But at least then I wouldn't have to hear my Father yell at me anymore.

Or I would hear him yell at me for an eternity.

I didn't know what it was really like in Tartarus—whether it was like the Hell that everyone described it as. Was it just darkness or was it seeing your worst fear again and again? I didn't particularly want to find out though, especially as that meant I would have to experience it.

I thought about a way I could try to sneak in lessons on controlling my powers. I needed to be somewhere safe—somewhere where I couldn't hurt anyone.

Oh wait, this was the Underworld, there was practically no one in the Palace.

I wondered what would happen if I accidentally hit one of the human souls that lived in the palace with my power. I remembered seeing Huntley's skin after I had an episode and there were dark marks on it, even though he was technically dead. I didn't quite understand how that worked and didn't want to find out the hard way.

Hermes seemed like he didn't quite fear what my power would do, trusting that I had control over it. He was a little naïve on that front. I mean, I was a lot better, but if he had seen what I had done to Poseidon…

That still made me smile a bit. I had overpowered him completely and made him suffer for what he was planning on doing to me. It made me sick to think of it.

And it made me realize it was the same thing Zeus had planned…

I pushed the thoughts back. Ugh, it made me sick. I had to figure a way out of this, and maybe my original thought was right—maybe I should figure out my powers so I could take him out somehow.

I took a deep breath and let it out slowly. I needed to walk around either way and get this energy out of me. I wasn't going to be falling asleep anytime soon—not with all these thoughts rolling around in my mind. I would just stay around the area and if Hermes ran into me, I didn't really care at this point. So what if he told Zeus, what would he do? Marry me?

Although I didn't quite care if Hermes thought that I was planning something, I did care that Father might find out and say I was careless and get into another big argument. I was still upset about the last argument we just had.

I didn't get why he was being this way. I thought that maybe he would understand by now, but I guess I was wrong. I wanted to be here, helping him, but there was no way that was going to last forever. Was he just upset it was by accident? Or did he think I did it on purpose?

I still wasn't sure what his reasoning was and wished that he would sit down with me to have a rational discussion, but I knew that wasn't going to happen any time soon. Not after what I had just said to him. Damn, I was a fool for yelling back at him. I guess I just let my temper get the best of me. And Mother. So pretty much I was screwed.

Wondering if it really wasn't possible to run away from Zeus, I thought back on any story Mother and

Father told me about the gods and if any of them were able to hide from Zeus. I couldn't think of one that was successful. The only place that people could potentially hide and get away with it was the Underworld, however everyone already knew I was here. I could try to hide somewhere else in the Underworld, however Father would be able to find me without a problem. So where was a place I could hide where no one could find me or go after me?

There was only one place I could go where no one could get me, and that was Tartarus.

Which was stupid to even think of, as no one has come back from Tartarus, I would pretty much be committing suicide and risking eternal torment. But I was the goddess of life and death, so would I be able to step foot inside the area if only for a little while? I knew that if I were sent there by Zeus, pretty much killed and trapped there, I wouldn't be able to escape. But what if I went there of my own free will? Would I be able to come back out then?

I pondered on this thought. It was curious to me whether I could go in and out of Tartarus if I in fact was the ruler over this domain. Could Father go into Tartarus without incident?

It wasn't an easy question to ask either, especially since then he would know where I was hiding, or at least figure out why I was asking. So Tartarus was theoretically a possible place to hide and maybe wait for all of this to blow over…

No, that was probably the stupidest idea in all of

existence.

The other problem was that if I was wrong, would there be any way to save my ass from Tartarus? I didn't think so, although many believed my power could surpass Zeus', so maybe I would be able to save someone from Tartarus one day. I thought about the moment where Zeus tried to kill me with his lightning bolt that Father was able to deflect. Would I have been able to survive that if it had hit me? Why was Father able to block it? There were still so many questions I had, but no one to ask.

How would I even test whether I could survive Tartarus? Ugh, this was frustrating me and making it so I couldn't fall asleep even more. I decided now was a time better than ever to roam around.

Hermes might found out, but by now I really didn't care. It wasn't like I could do anything. At first it was a worry, but now I just needed to move around and get some fresh air.

Getting up and putting on a robe, I stepped outside of my room. It was quiet, and I didn't hear Hermes getting up out of his bed to see if I was doing anything. The hallway was dark, only low blue lights bringing shadows across the walls and floor. It was eerie, I had to admit, and I didn't particularly like walking around the Palace at night because of it. It was hard to explain, especially since it wasn't like I was afraid of ghosts—I lived in the Underworld after all. But something about that light freaked me out.

It really freaked Huntley out as well, especially when

Father appeared out of nowhere and scared him. Father never showed it, but I knew he thought it was funny to watch Huntley scream like a little girl.

Letting the memory drift away, I took a slow breath and closed my bedroom door behind me. As quickly and quietly as I could, I headed towards the balcony.

The best thing I found out was that the Underworld was always the perfect temperature. When we were in London, I found it to be rather cold and uncomfortable at times. Although I always wanted to see the changing of the seasons, which all happened thanks to my mother, I did like always feeling comfortable.

The warm air felt nice against my skin and I closed my eyes as I leaned forwards against the railing. Life felt stuck and crazy at the moment and I wasn't sure what I should do. The idea of Tartarus was still running through my head, although it wasn't the greatest plan I had. It was probably worse than going to Earth. Or maybe even just a close second.

Opening my eyes, I held up my hand and let the energy be released from it. It cracked in the sky, dark tendrils going every which way. It felt good to let it all loose as it felt like it had been pent up for some time.

Sometimes the power was overwhelming and made me want a little more. It was like a craving for something that couldn't be explained. I quickly let it all go and took a deep breath. I had to keep reminding myself not to be carried away, or I would really raise some questions.

I wasn't quite sure as to how my power over life worked. The only time I had used it was by accident both on Huntley and A.J., but also Poseidon. Before then, the only power I understood was that of death. How did one control life? I supposed my mother would know, but she wasn't really someone I would want to talk to about it.

Out of spontaneity, I jumped up on the railing and peered down at the empty hole that was Tartarus. It was dark, as if it would go on forever. There were souls falling down from the sky of Earth—plummeting down into the giant never ending space. They seemed so close that I felt like I could touch them. Although I have always been curious, I never had stuck my hand out to touch them.

I wondered what it would feel like…

I reached my hand out to see if I could touch them—to see if I could feel the coldness of their souls. I thought maybe it felt like rain. I was wrong though, as I stuck my hand out and I felt something grab hold and pull me straight down, not letting my hand go.

I slipped off the balcony and headed down, screaming.

Chapter 18

<u>Huntley</u>

Pothos and I never stopped running until we were back to the flat. My heart was racing what felt like a marathon as I collapsed on the ground. Pothos fell down as well. Well, at least I didn't feel like a complete loser human for wanting to pass out since he was worn out as well. I glanced over to him to find his eyes closed and his chest moving up and down quickly.

Neither of us spoke a word for a while and just lay there in silence. I thought back to the woman I had seen earlier today. I could have sworn it was Persephone. A little part of me thought that maybe it had been Persephone and she had used her godly powers to make herself look different. It was possible, I knew, but whether I was right was another story.

I thought for being a human with all these gods, I was doing pretty well. I didn't have powers like they did, didn't have the centuries of knowledge they did, yet kept up with them, or at least the ones I've met thus far. Sure, I wouldn't able to actually fight them or be able to even hold out through the fight, but at least mentally I felt as if I was keeping up with them.

My mind traveled to the end of our search today. Ares… was scary. I didn't want to cross him ever again. *Like* ever again.

I was really glad that he seemed to be on our side. The moment he heard about the marriage he seemed really pissed. He didn't question us about the daughter of Hades or anything about that, but really focused on the second marriage. I wondered why that was. I didn't know much about the god, other than he was the god of war and I could now understand why.

"Hey Pothos," I said, still gasping for air. "Why was Ares so upset?"

Pothos opened his eyes and rolled over. "That is a long story."

"Don't have anywhere to go currently."

He sighed. "Fine, let's sit on the couch and I will tell you about him."

It took all of my strength to stand up. My legs felt like jello but I managed to stumble towards the couch and collapsed on it.

After taking a few deep breaths, Pothos went on with his story. "So you know how I used to live with

Aphrodite?"

"You mentioned it, yes."

"Well, Aphrodite and Ares fell in love with each other and wanted to marry."

"Shut up," I said. "The God of War and Goddess of Love?"

"Yup. Anyway, Zeus hated their relationship and made Aphrodite marry Hephaestus. Aphrodite protested as she hated Hephaestus, but you know how Zeus can be when he gets an idea in his head."

"I've noticed, yes."

"Anyway, he wanted to marry Aphrodite anyway, but Zeus wouldn't allow more than one marriage to a god, so Aphrodite and Ares never married and she is stuck in a loveless marriage. I mean, of course Ares and her have affairs all the time, Aphrodite has a lot of affairs all the time, but it isn't the same for Ares. He wants her all to himself."

"The more I hear your guys' stories, the more I find Zeus to be a giant dick."

"Welcome to the family."

I laughed, even though I knew it was true and in the end it wasn't actually that funny. It just had been a really long day.

"And what about you?" I asked. "He seemed to hate you on the spot. What did you do?"

Pothos shrugged. "I guess I just pushed a few buttons for both of them where I shouldn't have. It wasn't on purpose, but sometimes my powers get the better of me."

"You slept with Aphrodite?" I asked. I didn't really care one way or another but was trying to put these weird pieces together.

He shook his head. "No, no, I wouldn't cross Ares in that way. But when he is over I've made him have some... intense dreams, along with Aphrodite. Apparently I crossed a line tapping into their mind like that and was asked to leave the consort for a bit."

I didn't quite see the problem with that, but didn't want to press for more information. Pothos didn't seem like he wanted to talk about it anymore.

"Well then, now what should we do?" I asked. "I feel like we will never find her in this city."

"Be patient, if we don't find her right away we can start asking around. I'm sure Prometheus knows some people."

"And use that potion of his?"

He nodded. "Yup. I'm surprised that Hades would trust him with something like that—he's never trusted anything with anyone before."

"Probably just desperate."

"Must be very desperate. I've never seen him like this before, although I haven't really seen him ever. It's not like he ever leaves the Underworld."

"Yeah, Zeus didn't think he would even come save his own daughter," I commented.

"To be honest, I didn't think he would either. I'm curious as to what stakes he is willing to go to save his daughter. I guess time will tell."

I couldn't see there being any way Hades would stop

from saving his daughter. I wondered why everyone thought it to be strange. He had sacrificed so much before she had come to Earth and I couldn't see him giving up without a fight for her marrying Zeus. I wished I could talk to him—to see what his plan was. All I wanted to do was help.

Which was exactly why I need to find Persephone.

"So you think Persephone is anywhere around?" I asked, sighing.

"Nope, probably not. Demeter and Persephone aren't around after you disgraced them like you did, you idiot." He was joking, but I really didn't feel like hearing this right now.

"Hey, how was I supposed to know that we'd need them days after I said that to Persephone?"

"I already said, you shouldn't ever piss off one of the great gods, or any god for that matter if you can help it. As for pissing off lesser gods, that's a little iffy. It depends what they are in charge of."

"So pissing off you is fine?" I asked with a bit of a smirk.

He folded his arms. "Yeah, and I will just give Chrys what she wants again."

I thought about punching him, but I knew it wouldn't do anything to him. He laughed, seeing my face redden with anger.

"You get way too angry, dude, you just need to learn how to chill."

"I will learn how to chill when I'm not dealing with any of Zeus' shit."

"Well then you will never be chill because he is always causing shit."

That definitely seemed like the case. So far everyone's story seemed to come to an abrupt close because of Zeus.

A few moments later, the door opened and Prometheus and Mel stepped in. By the look Prometheus had, they hadn't found anything either.

"Let me guess, you two just went and had sex somewhere while the rest of us searched all day." I knew that probably wasn't true, but the way Mel was all over him, I had to make that comment. She was more annoying than when it was just Pothos, her, and I, which was saying a lot. At least she was out of our hair and in his constantly.

She grabbed Prometheus' hand. "No, silly. We finished asking around for her and are back here to have sex."

As she pulled Prometheus up the stairs, Prometheus added, "we didn't find anything. Apparently, her and Demeter had an argument and Demeter went back to Olympus. As for Persephone, well, she pretty much disappeared. No one has heard from her since."

"Wait, who did you—" I began, but the door slammed shut. I rolled my eyes and turned to Pothos. He simply shrugged.

"Don't look at me, I don't get involved with those two anymore."

"Whatever" I said. "At least we know she isn't in Olympus. Now we just have to figure out where on Earth she is. This isn't that big of a place, right?"

Pothos laughed. "Yeah, keep telling yourself that. We

can keep searching at least, but we have to make sure the wrong people don't overhear us asking about Persephone."

"Because of Zeus, right?"

Pothos shrugged. "Yeah, him, but I'm thinking of someone else, actually."

I gave him a look. He had never mentioned this before. "What do you mean? Who is scarier to get involved with than Zeus?"

"Well…"

As if on cue, the doorbell rang. We both stared at the door, wondering who it could be. I glanced over at Pothos, who looked more scared than I had ever seen him.

He shook his head and smiled. "No, that would be way too coincidental. There's no way it's them. It's probably just some Mormon or Jehovah's Witness missionary. It has to be."

The doorbell rang again. We both stared at the door.

"Are you going to get that?" I asked.

He shook his head. "No, I'm going to wait for them to go away."

"What if it's Persephone?" I questioned, though I doubted it.

"Believe me, it's not."

"Ares?" I asked. For a moment we were both quiet.

"If it's him, he would be shouting already so I'm going to say it's not him."

"Then who are you afraid it might be?"

He shrugged. "Don't worry about it, it's not them.

They haven't been seen me for quite some time."

"Who?" I asked yet again, even though I knew my question wasn't going to get answered. Pothos just looked at me, biting his lip. The bell rang again.

"Yeah, I'm not answering that. I feel like I jinxed it by even almost mentioning their name."

He was superstitious? Really? It made me want to know who he didn't want to run into even more. "Then what should we do?"

"Wait for them to *go* away. Then hide in here until we know for certain it wasn't…"

"Wasn't what?"

The door exploded into what seemed like a thousand pieces. Splinters of wood went in every direction. I took cover behind the sofa with Pothos as he was cussing up a storm under his breath.

The noise was loud, almost like a bomb. Even though only a few seconds had passed, it felt like minutes and I wondered how Prometheus wasn't down here already, wondering what the commotion was.

I waited until the debris cleared before I looked up and over the couch. There were pieces of door scattered in every direction, most of it embedded in the wall and couch. Pothos looked as if he were going to shit bricks.

As I examined the room, I noticed that there were three figures in the doorway. As they stepped inside, I saw that they all had gorgeous red hair, fair skin, and looked as if they had stepped off of a model runway. They had to be something mythological because beauty like that didn't come naturally.

"We heard you have been asking about Persephone," one of the three girls smiled. "Now, we have to know, who's asking?"

Chapter 19

<u>Chrys</u>

Shit shit shit shit.

I was falling fast. The soul, or whatever it was, that I had touched pulled me further and further down. Damn it, why had Father never told me not to touch the stupid souls? You would think he would have pointed it out, or maybe he just thought I was smarter than that. Well, he should have known by now that I was clearly not making good decisions for myself. I was royally screwed.

What was happening? Which way was up? Why was it able to grab me?

I had a feeling that this wasn't normal—that the soul should not have been able to grab me. If that was the case, though, then what had a grasp on my wrist?

I tried to look forward, to see what it was, but I couldn't see anything but the souls that were around me, trying to grab at me—but none of their touches I could feel.

So it wasn't a soul that had me.

As I fell further and further down, I tried to figure out what to do next. I had no way of stopping, nothing to grab on to. So I would just have to fly out of here.

There was a problem with that, mainly that I never really learned how to. I knew I had flown out of the water when I was fighting Poseidon, but that was it for me. Father never showed me how to use that part of my powers. Hell, he hadn't even taught me to use any of my powers. All that I figured out so far was on my own.

I tried to just think about going up, about getting away from falling down into Tartarus, but I didn't feel anything. It was as if whatever was pulling me down was even stronger than I was. There was no hope in getting out of here the way I was going now.

I tried to scream, but my voice wouldn't come. There was no sound, not to mention nothing would hear me out here. Now I really was beginning to panic, wondering if I would really get out of this or suffer eternal torment.

There was no one around to save me either. Both Hermes and Father were probably fast asleep, dreaming away while I fell straight into an abyss. It was starting to get colder, but not like a temperature change, but more a lack of anything substantial. It was like complete and utter darkness had a grasp on me. I couldn't imagine spending eternity here, especially when I hadn't even come close to being near the bottom.

I tried to use my power again, but nothing worked. I couldn't summon anything, fly, I practically couldn't do anything. I flailed a lot, which caused some spinning and then made me sort of dizzy.

Screams of the surrounding people echoed through the area. I swore I could almost hear laughter, deep and thick coming from the bottom of the pit, although I still couldn't see where that was. The sound felt like it was consuming me, wanting to destroy me.

Was this Kronos?

I took a deep breath and tried to focus on it, tried to really understand what it was. It was the only thing I could do at the moment.

Whatever it was had to be powerful, more powerful than anything I had ever felt before. It was dark, overpowering, and I could barely even think straight with it trying to surround all my senses. It wanted control over me, but I knew I couldn't let it.

It was Kronos that had grabbed me. This wasn't an accident, but something deliberate. He saw my weakness and took me by surprise. This was my grandfather trying to seek his revenge by destroying me.

Inexplicably, this thought made me focus, made me understand what I needed to do. I placed my hand forwards and concentrated on the darkness. I could defeat it, I could throw power straight ahead making me push myself back up to the palace.

I concentrated, sensed where the darkness was coming

from. They always said to fight fire with fire, and I guess this was my way of doing it. If he thought he had more darkness than I; well, he had another thing coming. The recoil should work, I prayed, and if I could just get close enough to the railing, wherever it was above me, I could save my own ass.

I let the anger and fear consume me, letting go of any restraints I had placed to keep the darkness at bay. Something felt different in the energy coming from below, as if it realized what I was doing and wasn't quite sure what would happen next.

Yeah, buddy, you weren't ready for this, were you?

I had gathered up all the energy, and let it explode from my my entire body, sending it down. Kronos backed away and let go of his prey. I had a feeling it would only be for a brief second. I felt my body shoot in the opposite direction. And for a moment, I thought it had worked—I thought that I was going up.

Was it up?

Now I wasn't sure. Everything felt like it was spinning around. Panic took over and pretty soon my energy was going in every direction. The surrounding souls didn't seem to be affected and I wondered if it was because they were already in Tartarus.

The more my fear took over, the more energy seemed to follow. It was going in every direction. It felt like shooting a laser blaster, spinning out of control in space. It wasn't doing any good but I couldn't stop, the fear and anger was escaping me.

Just then, I felt something grab around my waist.

I let out a scream and felt the energy emanate in every direction of my body. Whatever it was seemed to falter for just a minute, then start to pull me.

Wait, was it pulling me up?

I peered towards whatever it was that had grabbed me to find Hermes with massive angel wings. It was him? How was that even possible? How did he know where to find me?

And how did he survive that burst of energy I had just sent out?

It took a while, but we finally reached the balcony where I had been pulled off of. Kronos never tried to grab at us and it felt as if Hermes had no problem flying upwards—he had wings after all.

Setting me down, we both collapsed onto the stone floor. It felt good to be able to catch my breath again. I didn't realize that the air had changed and now this fresh air felt so much better. I glanced over at Hermes, whose wings slowly disappeared.

And I could see the black marks that covered his body —the black marks that I had caused.

"Are you—" I began, but he interrupted me.

"What in the name of Zeus were you thinking?"

I shook my head. "It's not like that, I didn't jump. Something pulled me down when I was up here on the balcony."

He stared at me, his face wet with sweat. "What are you talking about?"

I shook my head. "I don't know, something grabbed my wrist as I was standing on the balcony looking down at all the souls."

"You are crazy, a soul could never grab a god in there. It had to have been something else."

He was right—it was something else. But I didn't want to tell him what I knew it had to have been. Kronos. As for why I didn't want to tell him, I wasn't sure. Maybe it was because of the power I felt and feared. "I don't know what, but that sort of scares me."

Hermes whispered under his breath, something about Hera. I didn't comment on that as I didn't want to think of how angry she could be that I was marrying her husband. That was a whole other issue I was leaving for later to deal with, if I even had to deal with it in the first place. My more important task was to get out of this wedding.

We sat there in silence, still processing what we had just gone through. Hermes looked like he was in pain, parts of his body almost appearing as if they were decaying.

"Hermes, I'm—"

He held up a hand. "It's fine. It wasn't completely your fault. I knew what I was getting myself into when I took this assignment. I just didn't think it was going to hurt this bad."

I took a deep breath and tried my best to not say I was sorry again. But I was. I truly was.

"So what now?" I asked him, trying to figure out what page we were on in this mess.

He slowly stood up, grimacing with every inch. "You are going to make up with your father and tell him what happened. We need to figure out if someone was trying to murder you or not."

"No."

He looked at me like I was crazy. "What did you say?"

I stood up and realized how sore my own body was. I thought about reaching for the railing but didn't want to go any closer to it at the moment. "I said no. I'm not telling my father what happened. It wasn't someone trying to murder me, it was just a weird accident."

"An accident that almost made you get trapped permanently in Tartarus!" I hadn't heard Hermes shout before and was a little surprised by it. But I wouldn't budge.

"I don't care. He can't know I almost screwed up again, okay? I just don't want to hear it from him anymore. We can figure it out on our own."

Hermes stared at me for a moment, then sighed. "Fine. You don't have to tell your father. But he's going to ask where the hell I got all these marks from."

"Just say you spooked me and I lost control."

He raised an eyebrow. "Really? He would buy that?"

I shrugged. "It may have happened before..."

"Duly noted, don't scare you. I wished I learned my lesson that way instead of what just happened."

I glanced over at the waterfall of souls. "Yeah, me too."

Chapter 20

Huntley

Who the hell were these chicks?

I examined each of the women, all three of them having the same hair—red with loose curls—but each of them seemed completely different. They reminded me *of Mean Girls*, or any movie that had a bitch and their posse.

The main woman was of medium height, had very dark red lipstick, and looked liked she would love to rip your heart out. Literally. She had a devil of a smirk on her lips and I could see her being a man-killer.

And knowing the Greek Mythology like I did, it was quite possible.

The other two were completely different. The shorter

one, twisting her curls around her finger, had a cute smile that screamed "yandere". She looked like she would giggle when she drove the knife through your throat, splattering herself in blood. As for the tallest of the three, she appeared as if she was here for solely business and nothing was going to change her mind once she decided to take a job.

But damn, were they sexy. The clothing they wore stuck to their skin like a well-fitted glove. They each had long-sleeved black dresses on. I couldn't help but just stare.

"Shit," I heard Pothos sigh. "We're screwed."

I glanced over at him for a moment to see what he meant when I felt a soft, firm hand grab my chin and forced me to turn back. The first woman who had spoken, what I gathered to be the leader, forced me to look straight into her eyes.

"Focus on me, sweeties, there is no one you'd rather talk to than us.". Her eyes were dark, ruthless, and if she was as powerful as her gaze was, then I agreed with Pothos. We were totally screwed.

"I... I don't even know who you are," I said. It was the only thing I could come up with, and, to be honest, I wanted to know who my killer was before I got slaughtered.

She laughed, her voice seductive and almost music-like. I could listen to it forever. I shook my head. What was I thinking? Why did her laugh all of a sudden make me forget everything around me?

She answered, "We are the three Siren sisters and

protectors of Persephone. Now, I will ask this again: what business do you have with our lovely goddess?"

I didn't know what to say. First, a Siren? Like a Mermaid? That would explain the sexy yet murderous look they had about them. But where were their fishtails? That was what Siren's had, right? And what did they mean by being the protectors of Persephone? That didn't quite make sense to me, but I was still new to this Greek Mythology thing.

But I did know that Sirens liked to kill.

I heard the door open upstairs. "Pothos, is everything alright?"

It was Prometheus. He took a lot longer than he should have after that explosion. The door was in pieces, for crying out loud.

He reached the bottom of the stairs and was wearing a white sheet wrapped around his waist. The moment he saw the three girls at the bottom of the stairs, he quickly turned around and ran back towards his room.

"Prometheus!" The main Siren who held my chin yelled up to him. "Come back down here now!"

Prometheus came back down into view, his face full of dread. The fact both him and Pothos were so scared of these three women made me even more worried. But if I were killed then I would see Chrys again, right? But on the other hand, I could just be eternally tortured... I didn't really know at this point. Even having been dead, I still didn't know what dying would be like. As it was more complicated than simply Heaven and Hell. Go figure.

"Well, well, Prometheus. Long time no see."

He glared at the woman who still had my chin in her grasp. "What are you doing here?"

"What do you think? You've been going around asking about my girl. A couple of gods contacted us, including Ares. You know the rules, if you have any business with Persephone, you have to go through us first."

Pothos, who was now standing near Prometheus, leaned towards him. "Oh by the way, we ran into Ares. Was going to tell you after Mel released you but as you can see, we now have company."

Prometheus sighed, either from just seeing the Sirens or that we hadn't told him about Ares. "Thelia, I'm so sorry, I seemed to have forgotten the rules. We knew she was around this city and just wanted to speak with her. I didn't think that meant I would have to go through you all."

"Oh really?" she unclenched my chin, her nails scratching my skin lightly. I rubbed it, trying to unclench the muscles I didn't know I could tighten like that. She stepped a few steps closer to Prometheus, her hips swaying back and forth as she walked in her four-inch heels. "Then explain to me why you went out of your way to make sure we didn't find out."

"Well apparently, we didn't do it well enough, did we?" Prometheus glared at Pothos, who threw up his hands. Apparently because we ran into Ares, this was happening. Great. But at least he didn't beat us into a pulp like I thought he would. Then again, I wasn't sure what these women were going to do.

Prometheus turned back to Thelia with a little smirk. "But now that you are all here, why don't you tell us where Persephone has been hanging out lately?"

Thelia placed her finger on Prometheus's bare chest, twisting his hair with her finger. "Why don't you just mind your own business and rot in Tartarus for a few thousand years?"

Now Prometheus looked like he was just playing games with her. He almost seemed like he was enjoying the attention. What the hell was going on? "Harsh, Thelia, you are the worst."

She ran her finger through his chest hair. "You know I am anything other than the worst, or do I need to remind you?"

"Over my dead body!"

We all looked up the stairs to find Mel standing there, still in her black bra and lace underwear. I looked away quickly, not particularly wanting to see a woman other than Chrys like that, though I had to admit Mel looked really sexy at that moment. I just had to remember to either look away or keep eye contact. These gods were so awkward when it came to this stuff—it was worse than high school.

Mel quickly came down the stairs and shoved Thelia away from Prometheus. I stepped back, not sure what this catfight was going to entail, especially between a goddess and a siren.

Thelia smiled devilishly. "Bitch, you know whose he was first? Just imagine us in Olympus before you even existed."

The two other sirens stepped forward, the shorter one eyeing Pothos. He kept looking away as if trying to get his mind off of everything going on. I didn't blame him and wondered if the two of us could sneak away. With the other two sirens there, probably not.

Darkness like Chrys' began to swarm around Mel. Her eyes turned black as onyx and I took a few steps back, knowing exactly what was coming and didn't want any part. Damn, this girl was crazy when it came to romance. Thelia was beginning to open her mouth when Prometheus stepped forward, blocking Mel from doing anything rash, which I knew it was probably too late for.

"Ladies, please. This isn't the time. We have more important things to worry about, alright?" he looked back and forth between Thelia and Mel. They seemed to be listening, but I doubt he would change their mind about the fight. He was brave to be standing between them like that. "Right now, the four of us need to speak to Persephone. Where is she?"

Thelia laughed, bringing her finger up to her chin. It scared me how amusing she found all of this, and how her two friends were quiet during all of this. It was like they were there in case something went wrong, and it almost felt like something *always* went wrong. "Like I would tell you where she is."

Prometheus responded. "Hey now, I've never wronged Persephone, unlike other gods."

Thelia ignored the comment. "What business do you have with her, anyway?"

"It's about her daughter," I explained. "We need to

save her from Zeus."

Thelia was quick to turn to me. "Well, well, well, looks like the human has a crush on that little goddess. What a whore."

I clenched my fist. I was so sick of these gods and how they viewed Chrys, even though they had never met her before. What were they even going off of?

I couldn't hold back my anger. "Are you kidding me? You don't even know her. Why would you not care about Persephone's own daughter?"

Thelia shook her head. "She isn't our mistress' daughter, she is that wretched god Hades' daughter. We have known about her for a while and know how much she is cherished by that vermin of a god. Persephone has nothing to do with her. Persephone wouldn't have anything to do with Hades if she could help it. She was tricked all those years ago into a marriage that should have never happened."

Damn, all these gods were always out to put Hades down. But that wasn't what really grabbed my attention. They had known about her. Persephone had told them everything, yet Hades had told her to keep Chrys' existence a secret. Would she really trust these three to not tell Zeus?

So what was their deal?

"You don't know the whole story," Prometheus added. "She is innocent, especially compared to you all. She doesn't deserve what Zeus has planned for her."

I did not like how he said that. I really didn't want to think about Zeus and... Ugh, I felt sick just thinking about it. I would save her before that happened. I had to.

Thelia laughed. "You can't be serious, there isn't anything you can do to stop that, so give up. Or actually..." Her eyes turned into a glowing blue. "We will just *end it* for you."

The Sirens changed, and I meant changed. Their skin stretched, their teeth turning sharp and feathers appearing all over their bodies.

What the fuck?

I had no idea what was going on. Why were they turning into birds? But that wasn't my biggest worry— my biggest concern now was that their mouths were now open because a deadly sound was ringing out of their throats.

The siren's song.

I didn't know what else was going on in the surrounding flat, as the sound felt as if it was ripping my body apart. It seemed like millions of claws were tearing apart my chest and trying to take out my heart. I had never been in so much agony—not even when we went through the passage back to Earth. There wasn't anything I could do to make it stop.

Yet, after what felt like an eternity, it did stop.

"That's enough!"

At first I didn't even realize it had stopped, as the pain was still echoing through my body. When I finally came to my senses, I found Pothos, Prometheus, and Mel had already come back to their feet and were staring straight at the doorway. I turned to find Persephone standing there.

Chapter 21

Chrys

Hermes and I were sitting in the dining hall, eating lunch. Today Vincenzo had made a really amazing mac & cheese. To be honest, he got really mad at me when I called it that, but it was macaroni noodles with some cheese sauce… That's macaroni and cheese.

It had been only since yesterday when my whole ordeal of falling into Tartarus happened. I admit, I was still traumatized. I had almost died—not dead, dead but eternal torture "dead ." It had such a cold grasp on my insides that I didn't think it would ever leave me.

I knew it was my imagination, but it still freaked me out a little. I didn't ever want to go through that again. I wondered if Father had ever felt that same experience, or if he even knew that it happened. He reigned over everything in the Underworld. It would make sense that he would know.

But it did make me realize what kind of power both my father and Zeus had in order to keep something so powerful like that down there. It was terrifying to realize Zeus, who possesses power enough to trap Kronos down in Tartarus, was whom I was going to have to take down in order to get out of this marriage. At the moment it didn't seem possible, as I barely even survived falling down into Tartarus. I wasn't even sure how he managed to grab me off of the balcony like that—especially since it had never happened before.

There was no way I could defeat someone like that. What were the Fates thinking? I wished I could have talked to them more and asked for specifics, but they probably wouldn't have given me any. They liked to focus on their own things they found interesting, even if it wasn't what the person wanted to hear about. They would just say that I would defeat Zeus and marry Huntley.

Which meant I needed more practice with my powers.

I had no idea how I was going to do that, not after last night. Hermes was watching me a lot more closely, which made perfect sense—I had almost died. I had to just figure something out—a way to get away from him and go practice on my own. I had a while, though, and right now I needed to get over what had just happened, or more what *almost* happened.

I tried to keep myself distracted from Tartarus, and

Hermes did a good job at that. We never talked again about what had happened, but I knew he could see that it had shaken me up a bit and did his best to keep my mind occupied.

I was starting to feel thankful for him, in a weird way. I knew deep down that he was working for Zeus, but at the same time I felt as if he really did care about my well-being. I truly wondered if he would report anything to Zeus if I were to start practicing my powers. I didn't want to find out, honestly, as I would probably just end up being disappointed in him.

His wounds were still visible—black marks across his skin, but he didn't seem to care. I wondered how long it would take for them to heal, or if they would even heal. I felt horrible about it, but he insisted not to make a fuss.

As we ate our not actually mac-and-cheese, I listened to Hermes as he talked about some trouble he got into as a kid. His stories were stranger than anything I had ever heard of before.

"And then I switched all the hooves on the cattle, which made them walk backwards! Apollo was pissed!" He was laughing up a storm now. I laughed with him, not even sure how that was possible, to change the hooves and make cows walk backwards, but I wasn't going to ask. I was just going to roll with it.

"Zeus didn't even care since I was just a tyke. But I apologized in the end and had to put it all back in order."

I really wished Zeus wasn't in this story. I noticed he was in a lot of Hermes' stories and began to wonder how much say he had in everyone's stories. It seemed he was always making trouble.

"Apollo and I are best friends now. He brings it up every now and again, but more for a laugh. Those were the good ol' days."

I really wished I could have been there, growing up with the other gods instead of hidden down here, although I realized I would have been killed on the spot. There were a lot of ways my story could have played out, but the present was where I was now and I had to deal with it.

As we laughed at his story, suddenly the doors flung open. I turned to find Father standing in the doorway, worry apparent on his face.

"Father, what's—" I began when he hurried over and wrapped his arms around me. Fuck, Hermes told him.

He pulled himself back. "What happened? Are you okay?"

"I—I'm fine. Honest," I said as I raised my hands. "It was just a weird accident, but everything is good now."

He glanced over to Hermes. He must have seen the dark marks, for they were quite visible.

"Some staff saw what happened. I didn't get a full description of the events until just now. Thank you for saving my daughter."

Hermes shook his head. "I didn't do it for you."

There was an awkward silence between the two of them. It felt like it was almost half anger, and half sorrow. These two had some serious issues.

"Either way, Hermes, please leave us for a moment. I need to talk to Chrys about what happened. I need to hear it in in her words."

I thought Hermes was going to argue only to find him grab his food and leave us. That was surprising, to say the least. They always fought.

"Tell me, Flower, what exactly happened?"

I looked at him, surprised that he called me "flower". He hadn't used his affectionate nickname for me in a long while. It took me off guard. He was truly worried for me, even though everything was fine now.

"I really don't know. I was standing on the rail, looking down, when something grabbed me and pulled me down into Tartarus. I'm sorry Father, I had no idea that you couldn't touch the souls that fell into Tartarus, if I had known—"

He shook his head. "What are talking about? There is no possible way a soul could grab you or pull you down into Tartarus."

I stared at him. So I was right, it wasn't a regular soul. "Then what could have been?"

I heard someone's mocking laughter in the back of my head. It sounded like an elderly woman—almost like Themis.

How could that be? How would she be in Tartarus, not to mention in my head?

Unless she set me up to fall so that I would use my powers?

Hades shook his head and wrapped his arms around me again. "Whatever it was, it won't get you now. I have the Palace on high alert. They will always monitor and make sure no one can hurt you. I'm sorry that I wasn't there to save you."

"I'm just glad Hermes was there. I tried to use my power and—"

"It's okay, it's not your fault. He knew what could happen." Father squeezed me even tighter. "I'm so glad that you are alright. When I heard about it, I was terrified. To think that you could have been lost like that made me realize I have been a horrible father to you in the past few months. For that I am sorry. Please, Flower, forgive me."

I felt tears begin to form in my eyes. "I am sorry for everything that happened as well. It's my fault you had to come save me on Earth, I didn't know what I was thinking. You have gone to many lengths to make sure I was safe and I ruined everything."

He rubbed my head. "Shh, it's okay. I shouldn't have put so much pressure on you. I should have known you had to see the entire world and what it has to offer. I was stupid not to let you do it earlier. I could have figured out a way for you to travel to Earth without being spotted. I was selfish. Please forgive me."

I shook my head up and down. "Yes, Father, I forgive you. I just want things to go back to how they were. I want... I want Huntley back, Father. I miss him so much, I haven't had anyone to talk to." Everything was coming out now and I felt like a cry baby in my father's arms. "He was the best person I had ever meet. I was stupid for causing him all this pain. I just wish to see him."

"You will, Flower, you will. Don't think this is all over. We will figure out something—there has to be something to get this marriage cancelled. I will do everything I can and pull any strings that I must. There will be no way he ever lays a finger on you. Not while I am alive."

We stood there in silence and in each other's embrace. I felt protected now, as if nothing in any world could get to me. I knew deep down that this wasn't reality, but at the moment that's what it felt like.

I had finally gotten my father back and it felt nice.

Chapter 22

<u>Huntley</u>

So Persephone was in London, and she just saved our asses.

I wanted to hug her, to tell her thank you for saving our lives, but I still couldn't move. I was also afraid that if I went towards Persephone that one of the sirens would kill me on the spot. I really didn't want that to happen. Not after what I had just gone through.

"Persephone," Prometheus grinned and he shot a look at the sirens. "We need to talk to you."

Persephone nodded, knowing exactly what this was about. I prayed that we wouldn't have to convince her to help us. She had just saved us, so that meant she was on our side, right? Had Ares talked to her and told her what had happened? He seemed like he knew where she was hiding.

"You want a way to stop the wedding, am I right?" Persephone asked as she looked over to me. I don't think she realized I had been staying with Prometheus and the others. I wasn't just some human trying to do this all alone. "And you think I'm the only one who knows how to do that?"

Prometheus nodded. "Yes, and we talked to Dionysus today. He said that you might have something up your sleeve, if you are willing to get sneaky about it. So, the question is, are you?"

Persephone appeared as if she was thinking for a moment, then shook her head in defeat. "It wouldn't work, she's already engaged. There is no way you could outsmart Zeus."

"Are you sure about that?"

Everyone was quiet, waiting for Persephone to answer. She stood there, biting her nail. My heart was beating loud—either because I was waiting impatiently for Persephone to answer and help, or I was still nervous because the sirens were still in the flat. They each stood there, next to Persephone, waiting to attack anyone who stepped near her. I still wasn't quite sure what Persephone's connection was to these creatures, but for how they dressed and acted, it didn't really surprise me.

Persephone finally spoke. "It could work, but we would need someone to sneak into the Underworld. It would have to be someone who knows the layout well and can talk Hades into helping with this plan."

Everyone was staring at me, of course. I didn't care what I had to do, as long as it meant I would get to save Chrys. I nodded. "I'm in. What do I need to do?"

"You will have to find Hades without Hermes knowing you are there. From there, Hades will know what to do," she said.

"Hermes?" I asked. "How do you know he's there?"

"That's not important, but I do know for a fact that he's there guarding Chrys. Zeus isn't blind and knows that you are making a plan so he sent him there to watch her. But he will be paying attention more to Chrys than Hades, so you should be able to get past him."

"And if I don't?" I asked, dreading the answer.

"Just don't let him see you and you won't have to worry about that," she answered with a bit of hesitation. Great.

"So when I find Hades, what do I tell him?"

"Tell him we are going forward with the plan the two of us discussed. He's not going to like it—he's totally against it actually, but I have a feeling he will comply. It's not like we have any other choice."

"What plan?"

"It's a complicated plan, but since you talked to Dionysus, Prometheus, I presume you are willing to go forward with this trick?" she turned to him, waiting for an answer.

Prometheus nodded. "I'd do anything to help."

Persephone stared at him for a moment longer, as if wondering if this was a good idea, then turned back to me. "Huntley, take my ring and go back to the

Underworld. Do you know where Hades' study is? Go in there. He doesn't let anyone in there and there is no way he would let Hermes in. Wait for him there."

"But he keeps it locked," I responded more out of habit rather than an actual question. I had snuck in there enough times to know how to get in.

Persephone raised her eyebrow. "Really? I've seen you sneak in there before. You are lucky Hades never found out."

I felt my cheeks turn a little red. "Umm, what about Chrys?"

She shook her head. "Don't talk to her. If you do, you will have a higher risk of running into Hermes and it will all be over. Do you understand? You would run a risk of all of this being for nothing and ruining any chance of saving her."

I nodded. "Yes, I understand." It would be hard, I knew, to go to Hades' Palace and not go to Chrys' room. I really wanted to see her. The urge would probably kill me.

Let's be honest, I would probably end up trying to see her… But I wasn't going to tell Persephone that. I just would have to be extra careful of not being seen. If Hades never found out I had snuck into his study before, then there's no way Hermes would spot me.

Although, I never realized Persephone had seen me break into that room.

"Good, now," she handed me the ring and closed my hand around it, "go as fast as you can and come back here. When you get back, we will have all this cleaned up, now won't we ladies?" She turned her attention to the sirens. They all rolled their eyes. They didn't seem too excited about dealing with the mess they had created. At least I didn't have to deal with it.

They all rolled their eyes.

I turned to Pothos. "You will keep an eye on everything?"

The shorter Siren wrapped her arms around him. "Don't worry, we will take good care of your friends."

I would be a little worried about this if Persephone wasn't there with them. Although the look on Pothos' face wasn't convincing. I had to leave him here, though, as this would be our only chance.

"Okay, I will head out now. See you all in a few."

With that, I put on the ring and headed towards the River Thames.

A man in a boat was waiting for me when I got down to the River Thames. He appeared almost like a comedian from the 70s—all old and looking like he wished he had his youth back. I presumed he was Charon, mainly because he was wearing a robe like in the movies. Otherwise I probably would have stayed clear of him.

I stepped up to his boat and he stuck out his rowing oar. "None shall pass!"

That was weird... I held up my hand. "I have a ring."

He jumped down onto the land and took a closer look. "You sure do. Huh, weird time of year to be shuttling guests. Well, get in I guess."

I followed him into the boat. It rocked a little and I

imagined what it was like last time to almost drown, or theoretically I did drown since Chrys brought us back to life. That would explain why coming to Earth had been so painful.

"Now, sit down, relax, and enjoy the ride." Charon laughed as if he had said a funny joke.

Damn, I think almost drowning like last time might be easier than this. This guy was beginning to get on my nerves.

"How long is this—"

"And off we go!" Charon said as the boat flipped over underneath the water. I screamed, thinking that I was about to drown. I waved my arms around, feeling as if there was nothing I could grab on to. I thought about jumping but the thought wasn't there long enough to do anything about it. Only moments later, everything was fine and I could breathe again.

We were in the Underworld.

Charon laughed. "Gets the humans every time. I've even had some humans jump the boat, thinking that they could rough it out in the waters. Let's just say, they didn't make it, not when it was the flip between worlds. Always be cautious of that."

"But then why didn't you say—"

"I've had so many people come my way that had Persephone's little ring on, but not when she was on Earth. I'm sort of confused by that, to tell you the truth."

I knew that if I tried to answer, he would just talk over me at this point. I clenched my fist, wanting to punch him so badly. I couldn't though, that wouldn't help

Chrys.

I looked down and could see Hades' Palace. At least I had made it this far. My heart felt like it wanted to skip a beat. I was so close to Chrys, and here was a place where I felt truly at home, which seemed weird, but it was true. The Underworld was the only place I ever felt happiness. I knew this was definitely not the same for others, but for me that was the case.

It was going to be very hard to leave this place again.

"Well maybe Chrys is just turning into her mother and has sent for you to come and pleasure her. Am I right, is it that?"

I'm not going to punch him. I'm not going to punch him. This ride wouldn't take that long and I would be able to keep my anger down. Yes, I would do exactly that.

"I mean, it's about time. That girl is at that age, you know, or at least in god-years. We are all pretty old. Except for me, of course, I am a lot younger than most of the gods. I was created after Hades, although if you were wondering, my brothers are about the same age as me. Thanatos and Hypnos, maybe you have heard of them?"

I hadn't. It sort of made me realize that I didn't know a lot about Greek mythology. When everything was over and Chrys was safe, I was definitely going to have to have a breakdown on everything that went on in this world, and Olympus. Especially about sirens.

"You probably don't since you are on my boat. One is the god of death and the other one is the god of sleep. I think their jobs are rather boring compared to mine. I get to work closely with Hades himself. I'm his right-hand man, you know."

Oh my god, this was so much worse than almost drowning when Chrys, A.J., and I tried to go through the rivers by ourselves. I would take drowning any day rather than listen to this oaf blabber on and on. There was no way his comment about being Hades' right-hand man was true. I felt like even Hades would get sick of him quickly. Maybe that was why he was out here on the water instead of in the palace.

Hades was my kind of sneaky bastard.

I wondered if Hades would really trust me without whatever Persephone was asking of him. I presumed he would since he trusted me to tutor his daughter, or at least let Chrys convince him to let me tutor. Boy, was I surprised when I first met him and found all of this to be real. I didn't even know what to do at first but just stare at him. He was not impressed with me.

I was really surprised he trusted Prometheus with the potion to wipe memories. I guess if Hades could trust him, I could too. It was hard, as I didn't really have anyone in my life that I could trust except Chrys, but I would give it a shot.

Especially if it meant I could save Chrys.

Chapter 23

<u>Chrys</u>

A couple of days had passed and it was the greatest couple of days since before going on Earth. For once, after months of cold shoulders, he and I were talking again, and it pushed away all the thoughts of Tartarus.

Except when I was alone in my bedroom.

I helped work on judging souls with Father, with Hermes there in the corner, watching. I wasn't sure if he had ever seen the judging process, as he seemed to be focusing heavily on what was going on, along with staying silent. When we weren't working, however, he talked his head off, mainly poking fun at Father. Father dealt with it, though, so that we could hang out together.

Currently, we were spending dinner together, eating

the special ramen that the chef made for the evening. It was rather filling and I loved when Vincenzo experimented with different recipes like this. It made me wonder why so many people ate crappy food compared to this.

Even though Hades and Hermes argued back and forth, it was a lot less stressful than when Persephone was home. The banter was humorous, and I could tell even Father was having a little fun with Hermes, but wouldn't admit it. He would never admit something like that.

As we finished eating, Father got up. "I have a few things to finish up tonight. I will see you in the morning, Flower."

"See you in the morning, Father."

He left Hermes and I sitting there. I glanced over at him and shrugged. "Well, now what?"

"Up to you."

I tapped my finger on my chin. "I think we should go play with my puppy."

Hermes sighed. "Fine. But I'm not throwing the ball."

"He only almost bit your hand off. He's just a puppy."

"That is not a puppy."

I laughed. "Whatever you say. Come on, let's go."

We headed toward where Cerberus liked to hang out near my room. I grabbed one of the balls that Father had created for him and threw it down the hall. All three heads snapped at it.

Hermes stayed back, not wanting to get near Cerberus. I was surprised at how frightened he was of the dog, especially since he didn't seem to be afraid of anything.

"What is it that makes you so afraid of him?" I asked. "He's a really good dog."

He pointed at Cerberus. "*That* is not a dog! That is a creature of darkness."

"That's not very nice. Besides, he's the best dog I've ever had."

Hermes raised an eyebrow. "You've had other dogs?"

"Well… no, but that doesn't mean he's bad."

Hermes shook his head. "You are just like your father. He loves this thing as well."

I sighed. "Now you just sound like Mother."

We were both silent when the left head brought me back the ball. I was able to get him to let go and throw the ball again. There they went again.

"I think, deep down, Persephone loves you, you know."

I let out a slight laugh. "Deep down you say? It must be really, really deep down then. She hates it here, even though I had to stay here. All she does is argue with Father, and she really hates Cerberus. She never should have married my father."

"They were madly in love once, and I have a feeling part of the reason she hates it down here is so she can deal with being gone for so long, and so no one gets suspicious and finds you."

I looked at him, confused, as Cerberus brought back the ball. I threw it yet again. "What do you mean?"

He leaned back on the wall, folding his arms. "Well, if Persephone seemed to really want to be down here, then someone would be curious as to why. I know I would have. Then someone would have found you."

I shook my head. "No, that isn't the case. That wouldn't explain why she is such a bitch when she's down here."

"I didn't say it was a good excuse, but more just saying what it could have been. I'm probably completely wrong, usually am."

"I have been curious, though," I said as I watched the heads of Cerberus fight for the ball. "How did you never find me while I was down here? I mean, you have come down here a few times."

"Your Father must have made some sort of protection for me never to see evidence. Believe me, I was quite surprised when I found out the truth. It does explain a lot about your mom's change in attitude though."

I didn't like how he was blaming me for the way my mother acted about being in the Underworld—that I was the reason that my parents were in an unhappy marriage.

Cerberus spat out the ball into my hands. I chucked it down the hallway.

"Another reason I haven't run into you is because of Cerberus. You probably didn't realize your Father trained Cerberus to not let anyone near you, at least that is my bet. Any time I tried to come down this corridor, he would attack me."

I turned to him, smiling a little. "Really?"

"Yeah, he's given me a couple of nasty bites before. Almost took off my arm once."

I laughed. "Really? I never knew my father had Cerberus do that. Man, I wish I could have seen that…"

"Hey! That's not nice."

"Sorry, but usually he's pretty calm around people. I mean he takes souls to Tartarus, but other than that he's pretty calm. And when Huntley used to surprise him… Or A.J…"

"Yeah, I don't think that creature likes anyone other than you and Hades."

That was probably true. He seemed to be well-behaved to me but I then realized we didn't have that many people residing in the castle, at least nowhere Cerberus was permitted. I wondered if there was a reason for that now.

"So this Huntley fellow—"

"I'm not talking about him to you," I said before he could go on.

He shrugged. "Hey, I was just going to ask if you really cared about him. He's just a human."

"Yeah, well, I don't really see the appeal of gods at this point. Besides, he wasn't just a human but someone in the Underworld with me. Contrary to you gods, my lover can't leave me if they die since they are already dead."

Hermes seemed to really think about this for a moment. "That is a very good point, other than someone could send him to Tartarus."

"But they could do that no matter where they are," I commented. And really, that was true. I mean, I could be sent to Tartarus as well.

"True. Seems like you have thought about this for a while."

I shrugged. It wasn't like I didn't have the time. I had been stuck here by myself for three months before Hermes came to watch me. "Why did Zeus take so long to send you to watch me? Why did he all of a sudden not trust that I would follow through?"

Hermes let out a little laugh. "That is a complicated answer. It has to do a lot about what's going on in Olympus and on Earth, mainly Olympus. Hera isn't that happy that Zeus went off and decided to marry someone. She gets pretty jealous."

I rolled my eyes. "Great."

"Usually Zeus just fools around with women and Hera punishes them one way or another. You being the daughter of Hades sort of makes that harder for her, since she knows your father will come after her. Not only that, but when there's an engagement involved, the laws and punishments for getting in the way are quite harsh, even for a god."

That was not reassuring. That meant if Huntley or I figured out a way out of this, we could be severely punished. I didn't know what to do.

Hermes went on. "So Hera could be planning your demise, and also since Zeus figured your human friend would be trying to do something. He's been sending people after him but don't worry, none of them have really done much damage. Your human is quite a fighter."

My eyes widened. "What? Zeus has been attacking

him?"

"I mean, not really. He's more just trying to scare him. If he killed him, then he would be down here. No, Zeus just wants to threaten him so that he doesn't try anything stupid."

I couldn't believe what I was hearing. I had Zeus give Huntley immortality to keep him out of this, now he was going out of his way to threaten him. He had some nerve.

"I am curious, thought, what that human thinks he can do. There is no way he can go against Zeus. No one can."

I agreed with that, but I couldn't push back what Themis had told me about defeating Zeus. Was everyone wrong? Was it possible to take down Zeus? Was the prophecy true?

"Well, with that thought, I think I am going to go to bed."

The thought of bed made me yawn. "Yeah, I'm going to head to my room now, anyway. Goodnight."

He turned and started off. "Well then, goodnight."

I watched as he left and grabbed the ball from Cerberus. Throwing it, I watched as he galloped away. At least I got a moment alone for the day. I felt a little smothered today, but even as I stood here, I knew one of Father's guards was probably watching me. Father was evidently frightened after I had almost been pulled into Tartarus. He just didn't want to spoil our reconciliation by discussing theories surrounding why a soul would have the force or nerve to pull me down like that.

I still wasn't sure how that happened. I ran through it

again and again in my mind. What had pulled me down like that?

You will be more powerful than Zeus. You would have been able to climb out of Tartarus yourself.

It was that woman's voice again. Themis. Was it her? Was she testing me?

That was some evil bitch test if that were the case.

Just as I was about to throw the ball again, Cerberus' attention turned down the hallway. Each head started barking happily, and suddenly he tore down the hallway.

"Cerberus, what are you doing?" I called after.

He didn't listen, which was typical. I hurried after him to find him hurrying towards my room.

"What in God's name are you doing?" I asked.

Cerberus started scratching at my door. What could be in there that would make him do this? No one could enter my room except Father and Mother as it was my place to hide and Father had used his power to seal it.

Well, both them, along with A.J. and Huntley could enter my room.

With that thought, I quickly opened the door to find a dark-haired boy standing in the middle of my room.

"Huntley," I whispered.

Chapter 24

<u>Huntley</u>

Chrys was standing there before me, her hair pulled back in a ponytail, wearing a typical outfit of black jeans and a purple shirt. My heart was speeding up, as if this moment had finally come and I couldn't keep up with it.

I could see Cerberus outside, panting, happy to see me. I didn't think the creature would miss me, but I guess I was wrong. I was just glad he didn't make too much of a commotion or attack me for that matter.

Chrys quickly closed the door and ran to me, wrapping her arms around me. I wrapped my arms around her as well, not wanting to ever let her go. I held her tight, her warm embrace something I wish I could enjoy every moment of every day. I knew I needed to get her out of this place and wished I could grab her hand and run off to somewhere no one would find us.

But yeah, I lied to Persephone. I had to see Chrys, I couldn't come here without at least telling her we had a plan. And feeling her embrace.

She was the first to speak. "Oh my gods, Huntley, I missed you so much. Why are you here? How did you even get into the Underworld?"

I didn't let her go but spoke softly in her ear. "Persephone gave me a ring. Listen Chrys, we are going to get you out of this wedding, someway—somehow. I am supposed to get something from your father that could help us. I promise you that we will figure this out, okay? I will never give up."

Chrys shook her head. "If Zeus finds out, then you are a goner. I don't know if I can live if anything happened to you."

"Don't worry about that, okay? I owe you my life. Besides, I couldn't live with myself if you were married to Zeus. He's a horrible match for you."

She let out a sad laugh and was quiet for a moment, just letting our bodies keep each other warm. I wondered if she felt the same way as me and actually did love me, or if she was just scared and needed a friend's embrace. Either way, I would be here for her, no matter what she needed. I wanted to hold her tighter, to make sure that this wasn't a dream.

After a bit, I had to speak. I wasn't one for completely quiet situations. "You know that Charon sure talks a lot."

She laughed. "Yes, that's definitely true."

"How does your dad even stand him?"

She shrugged. "Huntley, that's not exactly something I really care to talk about right now. What I want to know is how you managed to sneak past all my dad's guards on top of Hermes."

Ah yeah, I knew she was going to ask me. Now I had to admit some things that I did while I lived here. What can I say—once a punk, always a punk. "Hermes was close. That's how I ended up in your room. I heard him coming around the corner and quickly jumped in here. Luckily, he wasn't able to follow me. As for your dad's guards, well, they all know me and I have bribed them a lot over the years, so they let me through without a sweat. Besides, they also knew I was coming to help you."

Chrys laughed again. Damn, I missed that laugh. I would do anything to hear it for all of eternity.

"You will be in deep shit if Hermes finds you. He's pretty smart and is constantly keeping an eye on me. For all we know, he could be keeping an eye on this door to see if you leave."

I put my finger on her lips. "Shh, don't worry about that for now, okay? I'll figure something out, I always do. I have snuck past your father countless times in his own palace—I can sneak past Hermes."

"How do you know my father didn't know what you were doing and let it go because he knew I liked you?"

She had me there. "I... I think he still would have talked to me about it."

She took a deep breath. "Fine. But please tell me,

what's the plan you have?"

I scratched my head. "Well, I don't completely know. I have been with Pothos, Mel, and Prometheus for a while and Prometheus contacted a lot of people which was then how we ended up getting help from your mom. She and Prometheus seem to have some kind of master plan, but only if I am able to get a box from your dad. No one really gives me the details since I'm just human."

"Sounds like gods. Anytime you come up, Hermes always puts you down for being Human. Also, my mother trusts Prometheus?"

"I guess? I mean, everything with her happened so fast, I'm not sure. She seemed to trust him, though."

She paused for a moment. "I don't know, do you trust him Huntley?"

Honestly, I didn't. However, I didn't want her to worry. "Yeah, I mean he has gone to a lot of trouble to help us and Pothos seems to trust him. I don't see why not."

"I guess when you put it that way. Just promise me you will keep an eye on him, okay?"

I kissed her forehead. "Damn I love you. I will, Chrys, I have been keeping an eye on him. I won't let him, or anyone, take you away from me."

"But it's better than Zeus," she whispered.

We stood there and I held her tighter. She was more afraid of Zeus than she originally let on. I could understand that. She was facing an eternity with a greedy god who was notorious for fucking every moving thing he saw. But I wouldn't let any man nor god take her away. Not unless he made her happy.

"Huntley…" Chrys began.

"Yeah?"

She looked up at me. "Can you promise me you will never let me go?"

I smiled. "Of course, whatever you want."

Chrys leaned forward and kissed me on the lips. This wasn't a gentle kiss either, but a strong one as if she had waited so long for this. Just like me.

I put my hand on her cheek, returning the passion. I had wanted this kiss for a long time as well. She was everything I ever wanted and I would do anything to make sure she was safe. That I knew for sure.

She pulled me closer, grabbing my shirt in her fist, and started inching towards her bed. I couldn't believe what she was inferring. I was right that she was inferring *that*, right? I mean, I didn't want to presume, but neither would I say no. It was a thought I had in the back of my head every time I saw her, to be honest. But I had to know. I stopped the kiss for a moment. "Chrys… are you…"

"Huntley, you may want to stop this wedding, but we both know the reality of the situation. This could be the last moment we ever see each again. Let's make it perfect."

I nodded slowly, not saying a word. I knew exactly what she meant. I kissed her again and let her guide me towards her bed. She pulled off my shirt and ran her hands along the skin of my chest. I took a long breath, letting the feeling linger on my skin. I grabbed for her own shirt and pulled it off as well. She was wearing a black lace bra that looked sexy against her skin. To be honest, anything she wore would look sexy.

Pulling her close, our skin touched and I kissed her strongly again. She pulled her hair band out of her hair and I ran my hands through her hair. It was soft and wavy and god I loved it. I moved my lips along her cheek and down her neck towards her collar bone. Chrys ran her hands down my back and pulled my hips closer to hers. I wanted this to last forever.

"I love you Huntley," she whispered in my ear.

"I love you too, Chrys." I kissed her on the lips again. She bit at my lower lip playfully, then pulled me on top of her bed.

This probably would end up being a mistake, but it was one I would happily make.

Chapter 25

Chrys

Huntley lay next to me, his skin sticky with sweat as was mine. I had finally done something that was on my mind since the day we met, but I could never act on it. There was the problem of ruining our friendship and him leaving me to go to paradise. I never thought he would stay for that long in the palace, but he did. Over the years together, we both had grown closer and I was glad I didn't treat him like my mother would have. I cherish our friendship more than anything, and now our love was something even more special.

I tried to keep my mind on the moment—to think time would never move and I could spend eternity with Huntley. But I knew the truth, what I was destined for.

The Fates had said that I would end up with the one I loved, but I didn't see how that was possible. I wouldn't give up between now and the wedding, though, but I also didn't want to have my hopes crushed. I was a realist, what could I say.

Laying my head on Huntley's chest, I played with his chest hair. "So…" I said. "That was fun."

He nodded quickly. "Yeah, it was like nothing I have ever experienced before."

I laughed. "I guess we gods are better than any human."

"That's for damn sure."

The warmth coming off his body felt great on mine. I wanted to stay like this for a little while longer, but I knew he needed to get back before Hermes found him.

"Huntley," I began. "How long will you stay here with me? I mean, I know you should get going but at the same time…" I trailed off, wishing I could go on and tell him to stay here forever, but that wasn't possible. We both knew that.

He didn't speak at first, as if realizing it himself that he couldn't just stay here. "Just a little while longer, okay?"

I nodded. "Yeah, a while longer would be good."

We lay there in silence, Huntley gently playing with my long hair. I thought everything was perfect until I heard a knock at the door.

Both of us froze. I could feel Huntley's heart rate speeding up. Dear gods, did Hermes find out he was in here? If so, we were screwed. My own heart was pounding in my chest.

"Flower, are you awake? I want to talk to you."

It was Father. Although better than Hermes finding us, I really didn't want to see what Father would do to Huntley. I had never had sex with anyone before and part of the reason is because of my fear of what my father would do, especially with a human.

I never saw Huntley move so fast. He grabbed his boxers and quickly put them on. I snapped my fingers and was dressed in purple pajamas.

Huntley whispered. "Can you do that to me?"

I shook my head. "No, I don't know how to do it on someone else."

He grabbed the rest of his clothes, cussing under his breath. "Shit, shit, shit."

Father knocked again. "Flower?"

I turned to the door. "Just a minute." I got up out of bed and shoved Huntley into the closet. "Hide in there." I shut the closet door behind him.

I ran my fingers through my hair a few times, then opened the door to find Father standing there, curious as to what took me so long. He stepped inside and closed the door softly, not to be heard by Hermes. We weren't supposed to have secret meetings like this, not without Hermes knowing. Although he has left us alone before, I knew he had been listening in. He wasn't stupid.

"Are you alright?" he asked. "You took a while answering the door."

I nodded. "I'm fine. Fantastic."

"I see." He gestured towards the bed. "Sit, I want to talk to you."

I sat down on the edge of the bed as he grabbed my desk chair and pulled it up. I watched as his eyebrows twitched and he looked like he was pushing back his anger. He took a deep breath, as if trying to stay calm.

"Huntley," he said as he turned to the closet door. "Would you please leave us so I can talk to my daughter alone?"

My eyes widened. "Father I can—"

He held up his hand. "I'm not going to kill him. I don't care right now, but I do want to talk to you alone."

The door to the closet opened. Huntley was still just in his underwear, holding his clothes in a bundle in front of him.

Hades just stared at him. I had never seen Huntley so scared in his life, and that included going against the gods.

"Sir, I—"

"Go to my study, the one you somehow figured out how to get into all these years and wait for me there. Watch out for Hermes, he's been wandering around tonight. Once you are inside, he can't open the door."

Huntley nodded and hurried out of the room. My heart was beating fast now. Shit, I did not want Father to find out about this. I wanted it to be a little secret between Huntley and I, especially since now Father was going to be pissed off at me again.

"Father..." I began.

He pinched the bridge of his nose. "It's fine. It's fine." He wasn't really saying it to me, but more to himself.

I decided to let him gather himself and tell me why he

was here. I don't think he wanted to talk about Huntley yet, or ever. Father took a deep breath again and looked at me.

"Flower, I want you to know that I will stop at nothing to end this engagement, okay? Your mother and I talked before she left and she has been gathering intel. I presume Huntley has a message from her and that is why he is here. I just want to tell you that you have nothing to worry about."

I couldn't believe what I was hearing. Mother was helping? Here I had thought they had left on bad terms, but now I knew the truth—they were trying to trick the gods into thinking they weren't on speaking terms so that Persephone didn't look suspicious.

"What are you going to do?" I asked.

He took a deep breath. "Well, I'm not a hundred percent sure yet, but we have a few plans. There is one in particular that your mother came up with, but I'm not too keen on it. It involved Prometheus and convincing Zeus that you are already married to him. Don't worry, you won't actually marry him, but it may make Zeus back off and since it's Prometheus, he doesn't believe the titan will cross him again and you will be watched closely. It's going to involve a lot of work on your mother's side to convince Zeus it is fine, but I think she can do it."

Persephone actually cared about me enough to go against Zeus like this? I was still in shock from Father saying that, that I didn't think twice about the plan.

I nodded. "Okay, I will do it."

"What I need from you now is to act like you are resisting, okay? I need you to try to escape a few times. If you don't do anything, it will appear that you are waiting for someone on the outside. It will make Zeus suspicious, especially if you are quiet. But nothing too drastic or Hermes will take you to Olympus. Got it?"

"Yes."

He leaned in and kissed my forehead.

"You aren't going to kill Huntley, are you?" I asked.

Father shook his head as he started opening the door. "No, don't worry. I won't kill him. Yet."

I didn't know if that was reassuring or not. I watched him leave and prayed Huntley wouldn't get caught by Hermes. I just hoped Mother and Father's plan would work, and that Prometheus would go with the plan, and more importantly, stay with the plan. Something in the back of my head told me not to trust him. Maybe it was his smile as it almost seemed selfish in nature. All the gods were selfish though, so I guess it didn't matter. It could be my only way for freedom, though.

That is, unless I could really defeat Zeus myself. That was a battle, though, I didn't want to happen.

Chapter 26

<u>Huntley</u>

I waited inside Hades' study, my clothes now on, and my heart racing like no other. I seriously thought he was going to kill me. I just had sex with his daughter and he found out. He was always suspicious of me, always thought I was up to no good, and now I proved him right.

Shit. Shit. Shit.

This was probably why Persephone didn't want me to see Chrys, knowing I would probably do something stupid like sleep with her and then get caught by Hades. He loved his daughter and saw her as the perfect child, and she was indeed perfect in many ways. Now I was the villain in his mind.

No, Zeus was the villain here. I had to realize that—I had to realize Hades knew that too. This was all to keep her safe from Zeus. Well, I mean, I didn't have to sleep with her in order to get her away from Zeus, but the point still stood. I was better than Zeus. Probably. Most likely. I was a decent human. I liked to think that I was.. Maybe not when I was alive.

Yeah, my mind couldn't think straight right now.

The door opened and my heart pounded even harder. Damn, it was hurting and feeling like my heart was going to give out. Hades stepped inside, his face cool just as normal.

I stepped forward. "Sir, I swear, I wasn't—"

He raised up his hand. "Huntley, what did I say? We aren't going to talk about it right now. We are figuring out how to stop the wedding first."

I nodded slowly. "Sure, whatever you say man." I mean, I didn't really want to think about it right now either. I was so glad he felt the same. Maybe it would all blow over and he would forget about it eventually...

Yeah, like that would ever happen.

Hades took a deep breath. "Now, I presume Persephone sent you?"

"Yup. She said you had a box in here that could help stop the wedding. Something for Prometheus?"

"I do," he said. "But I still don't know if it is a good idea."

"You don't trust Prometheus either?" I asked. "Then why did you give him the memory loss water?"

"I figured he could use it to help. It doesn't mean I

trust him, however. Huntley, promise me you will watch his every word. Persephone trusts him, but I don't really like her judge of character if you know what I mean."

I did know what he meant, especially when it came to those sirens. "Yes, sir."

"Good. But I do think it could be our only chance, even if it's a long shot. I mean, if all else fails, there's always war."

I didn't say anything. Was he being serious? A war between the gods? All the stories I did know, both of mythology and of fictional stories, a war of the gods never meant anything good.

"I'm joking. I wouldn't do that to the world. It is tempting though." He let out a sigh. "Let me get the box for you."

He pulled open a drawer and grabbed a little black box. "Now, make sure no one sees the contents of this box except for Persephone, you got that? And if it doesn't work, Huntley, will you promise me that you will stop at nothing to ensure my daughter's safety?"

Hades handed me the box. This was it? How would something in this tiny box ever going to help? I mean, I wasn't going to ask Hades that. He knew what he was doing. I nodded. "Yeah, I promise I will do anything."

"Good." He placed his hand on my shoulder and squeezed it quite hard. He looked straight at me, his eyes dark. "And when you get back from stopping the wedding, we can have a little chat about how you had sex with my daughter."

My heart practically stopped. "I thought you said we

weren't talking about that."

"No, I said we weren't talking about that at this moment. When this is over, we will be having a talk."

I nodded. "Sounds good. Looking forward to it."

He let go of my shoulder and narrowed his eyes at me. "Now get out of here and save my daughter."

"Yes sir." I went to open the study door to find a strange man standing there. Fuck, it had to be Hermes.

"Well, well, what do we have here?" he had a bit of a smirk on his face.

Shit. Shit. Shit.

Hermes examined me for a moment, then saw the box in my hand. "Oh, that is a good idea. Wonder if it will work. I guess only time will tell."

He looked over at Hades. They kept each other's gaze for a moment.

Hermes clapped his hands together. "Well, looks like I saw nothing here, now did I? I mean, I am just wandering around ma*king* sure no one has snuck in to hurt Chrys. Never said I was looking for anyone else. Guess there was really nothing to worry about." With that, he turned and headed down the hallway.

I had no idea what had just happened. Was Hermes helping Chrys? What the hell did I miss? I mean, Chrys was awesome and anyone who knew her wouldn't want harm to come to her. I guess it made sense, but still.

Hades shoved me forward. "Hurry up before he changes his mind."

I moved forward and headed to where Charon waited for me. I was so looking forward to another trip with him. Not.

***

I made it back to London after the painstaking journey with Charon. He was so boring. Oh my god. I knew it would be the least troublesome thing in this entire journey, but seriously, he was annoying.

I had the box in my hand as I stepped inside Pothos' flat. The door had been fixed by the sirens already, even though it had only been one night. Everyone, including the sirens, were still waiting for me, all passed out on the sofa and floor. The only one who was awake was Persephone and Prometheus. Prometheus stood up and came over to me.

"So it was a success?" he asked.

I nodded and made my way past him to hand the box to Persephone. I wasn't going to give it to anyone but her. She mouthed a 'thank you' and took it from my hands. Prometheus and I stood there as she slowly opened it. Inside were little red seeds.

Prometheus smiled. "Finally, we have the way that we are going to save the daughter of Hades."

Thank You For Reading!

Thank you so much for reading! Readers like you make it possible for authors like me to write stories! If you could spare a moment and leave a review on Amazon, Goodreads, BookBub, and wherever you like to buy books, that would mean the world to me! It really helps authors like me to succeed in the publishing world.

A big thank you again for your patronage. I hope you will check out the next book in the series and my other series. Keep reading to get a sneak peak of Book 3 of Daughter of Hades: Entangled!

CHAPTER 1

Chrys

Today marked my last day in the Underworld, as there were two weeks left before the autumn equinox. There had to be a way out of the marriage, and Huntley would find the means. Although I had the strength to free myself, I understood that my father would pay the price for my rebellion. Zeus might hurt my mother, father, or maybe even Huntley if I tried to escape. I wouldn't let that happen. No, I accepted my fate unless Huntley and the others found a loophole. He was a human, but he was smart and would go to the ends of the Earth to help me.

I enjoyed the summer months learning from my father, even if Hermes intervened whenever he wanted. Hermes stopped annoying Hades whenever he felt like it, but still got on Hades' nerves at least once a day. I stayed out of their feud, as I learned their argument was centuries in the making. Their interactions delighted me, though.

Father decided to put together a big dinner tonight. The dinner seemed odd to hold as the whole situation wasn't something to celebrate, even if it was for a wedding. My heart felt as if it skipped a beat every time I thought about leaving this place. I wanted more than anything to get out of this mess, but it was my fault this was all going on—I should have just stayed in the Underworld and never ventured to the mortal realm. Father almost died because of my mistake, and now I had to face the consequences.

During the last few months, I grew fond of Hermes and considered him a good friend, even if he was working for Zeus. I didn't have many friends to begin with, as I couldn't interact with other gods in fear they would report back to Zeus. The only friends I had were Huntley, Maka, and AJ, but AJ didn't consider me a friend. He just used me to get out of the Underworld. He lied to me for centuries, starving himself and acting like he cared for me.

The betrayal still burned, and I didn't think I could ever forgive him. It seemed like most gods were like that, though—not having the ability to forgive. I dreamed about getting my revenge on him someday, but decided he wasn't worth the effort. If I crossed paths with him one day, however, I doubted I could hold back my wrath.

I couldn't wait for that day.

Hermes and I were outside on the balcony, watching

the shimmer of Oceana glisten from the sunlight in the mortal realm, and the rainfall of souls into Tartarus. I could even see Charon in the distance, guiding the souls that Hades would judge himself. I wondered how many of the souls that went to Tartarus even believed that it existed. I had heard it all while judging with my father: I didn't know; I made a mistake; I was just a human; there were no signs. Any excuse they came up with was meaningless. They just said it to save their skin, not because they felt guilt. They should realize the God of the Underworld could see through their lies and into their souls. I guess if they were that smart, they wouldn't be on their way to Tartarus.

It felt as if Hermes was looking over at me instead of out to the distance, so I peeked over at him. I was right; he was staring right at me with his aquamarine eyes.

"What?" I asked.

He laughed and shook his head. "You and your father are a lot alike. Although I think you are kinder than he is."

I didn't think I was like my father at all—he was benevolent, a hard worker, but stern in a caring way. "No, he's a lot stronger than I am. He is a bold leader of this world and I can't even look at my future without trembling."

"I think that is where you are wrong. You are stronger than you realize. And besides, between you and me, he's always fearful. But that makes people strong," Hermes explained.

"What do you mean?"

"If you had nothing be afraid of—if you felt no pain —then what is there to be brave about? No, the ones who struggle the most are the strongest because they keep on going even against all odds."

I liked how Hermes could be sarcastic and troublesome one moment and compassionate and caring the next. Although I don't think I had ever seen him be compassionate when my father was around. I guess he only did that for me.

"Thank you Hermes, I needed to hear that."

"My pleasure. Now we better not keep your father waiting any longer."

I chuckled. "That's the first time I've heard you say that."

"Well, tonight is different. I don't want to push any of his buttons. Not for a while, at least."

I knew what he meant by that. I let out a sigh and followed him back into the dark-stoned castle. I would miss this place, as I doubted Zeus' home was a gothic-style castle like something out of Dracula. Although my mother always hated how brooding it felt, I loved it. I would still get to be home most of the year, when my mother was in the mortal realm. I made sure that was part of the deal as Zeus had forced the same when my father married. It was only three months of the year. That wouldn't be that awful, right?

As we stepped inside, Cerberus came running into the hallway, his three heads bouncing up and down. I didn't even need to kneel for him to lick my face. I would miss him while I was away, especially since I would know my mother would shrug him off and ignore him for the time she was here. She always seemed to loathe him, even though he was her pet. At least father would be here to spoil Cerberus as much as he could.

"That dog likes you," Hermes commented as I rubbed Cerberus' belly.

Cerberus turned and growled at him. I laughed. "He likes me, yes, but I thought by now he would have warmed up to you. I guess not."

"Yeah, well, I think your father has trained him to hate me."

"Fair enough, he probably has. I think I might have seen him whispering things in Cerberus' ear about you. If I were you, I wouldn't come down here unless I'm around just to be safe."

Hermes monitored Cerberus, who was still glaring at him. "I'll keep that in mind."

We headed down towards the dining room where a feast was waiting. I was curious what my father had prepared for the night. I wasn't even sure who would be there, especially since I didn't have that many people close to me.

Opening the door to the dining hall, Hermes ushered me inside. I gasped in astonishment at all the food that lined the table. It was every kind of food I had ever loved, including memorable dishes I had eaten when I visited London—scones and pots of tea. How he found out about me loving it, I had no idea. There was also my favorite German dish käsespätzle, crème brûlée, roasted veggies with herbs, and Black Forest cake.

My eyes were so glued to the food that it took a second to see the other people gathered around the table. Maka, the three stooges, Charon, Nyx, whom I hadn't seen in forever, and Hekate They were all here to see me off, even though I rarely saw them and leaving for Olympus would not change the amount of time I would see them. But father must have asked them to come and although I knew they would never go against a request of his, they would have come either way to see me off. I smiled and gave Maka a brief nod to tell her thank you. I couldn't remember the last time she was in the palace like this. She was typically far too busy, so it surprised me to see her on this side of the Underworld. They were all busy, to be honest, but they put their lives on hold for this last dinner before seeing me off.

Hermes pulled out the chair for me, and I took a seat. Everyone was so quiet that it was a little awkward. I didn't know what to break the silence. I feared that if I opened my mouth, I would weep. I glanced over at my father, who must have understood. He tapped his wine glass to call attention for a speech.

"Everyone, help yourself."

With that, everyone loaded their plates with the food father had prepared. Words and laughter filled the room as the gods and goddesses filled in each other on all the adventures they had since the last time they had seen one another other. From some conversations, it was clear some of these gods hadn't seen each other for centuries. Maka, who sat across from me, sipped on tea that I mused whether it was a type she had bought, or if my dad had made a special brew just for her.

"Don't worry, child, this is not the end. You are still a part of the Underworld, no matter where you go." She glanced over at Hades. "Just like your father."

"I know, it's just going to be hard to adjust is all. Everything of mine is here, and the times I'm gone I will miss the shimmer of Oceana. I have never even been to Olympus, I don't know what to expect."

"It's a beautiful place," Hermes chimed in. "It is filled with gold and clouds, and everything seems to be glowing."

Father interrupted. "Including people's egos. The land may be beautiful, my flower, but the people aren't. Everyone up there is ready to stab each other in the back, so be careful to guard yourself as I won't be there to keep you safe."

Maka placed her hand on his shoulder. "Don't worry, Hades, she will be fine. She is strong, remember? She went up against Poseidon himself. I doubt anyone will cause him any trouble."

"Man I wish I got to see that," Hermes commented. "There aren't many who can take him down. I would have sold tickets to all the other gods to watch and have made an enormous bowl of popcorn."

I saw the side of father's mouth twitch, as if he would

smile, but he didn't let anyone see he found it amusing.

"I'm still not sure how I did that, and also those powers are the reason…" I trailed off, not wanting to bring up the marriage with father there. It was still hard for him to talk about.

"So you will be with Persephone for the next two weeks, right?" Maka asked. "You will see what it is like for gods on the other side through her lens. I think that will be an interesting experience for both of you."

I shrugged, not wanting to talk about mother to her. I still wasn't happy with the way things ended with her and I didn't want to admit it. I was also not sure if spending two weeks with her would be fun or awful. If history repeated itself, which it did, it would be the worst experience of my life. But then I wouldn't ever have to see her again, at least not if I didn't want to. She would be in the Underworld while I lived in Olympus, and I would be in the Underworld while she lived in the mortal realm. It was a win-win for where our relationship was at the moment.

"And Demeter," Hermes added. "You have never met your grandmother, have you?"

I shook my head. "No, I have not."

Father mumbled under his breath so I only could hear. "Ugly old cow if you ask me."

I chuckled, and we gave each other a smile. I didn't know what to expect with Demeter, and could only imagine her to be like my mother, but worse.

"What did I miss?" Maka asked.

I shook my head. "Nothing. Don't worry about it."

"Probably something about Demeter, if I'm not wrong." Hermes took a bite of his steak. "Hades has never gotten along with her. Actually, he doesn't get along with anyone who isn't in the Underworld."

"That's because no one down here is a backstabbing liar."

Hades and Hermes stared at each other while Maka and I laughed. I didn't want tonight to end.

BUY ENTANGLED *ONLINE OR AT YOUR LOCAL BOOKSTORE*

Acknowledgments

I want to thank everyone who made this novel possible. A big thank you to my editor Justin Boyer who hopefully hasn't gotten sick of reading my stories yet. Thank you to Biserka Design for the amazing covers for this series! I love them lot! A special thank you to Dr. Almira Poudrier at ASU for answering my questions about Greek Mythology as things get weird and confusing and even more weird. And, lastly, thank you to my husband and parents who are always supporting me.

About the Author

Dani Hoots is a science fiction, fantasy, romance, and young adult author who loves anything with a story. She has a B.S. in Anthropology, a Masters of Urban and Environmental Planning, a Certificate in Novel Writing from Arizona State University, and a BS in Herbal Science from Bastyr University.

Currently she is working on a YA urban fantasy series called Daughter of Hades, a YA urban fantasy series called The Wonderland Chronicles, a historic fantasy vampire series called A World of Vampires, and a YA sci-fi series called Sanshlian Series. She has also started up an indie publishing company called FoxTales Press. She also works with Anthill Studios in creating comics through Antik Comics.

Her hobbies include reading, watching anime, cooking, studying different languages, wire walking, hula hoop, and working with plants. She is also an herbalist and sells her concoctions on FoxCraft Apothecary. She lives in Phoenix with her husband and visits Seattle often.

Feel free to email her with any questions you might have!
danihootsauthor@gmail.com